Lily picked up one of the magazines from the coffee table and opened it at random, and then wished she hadn't as she glanced down to find Trip's out-of-this-world face staring up at her from the page.

She felt a spasm of pain around her heart. It had been weeks now since Trip had gone missing.

The buzzer to her door rang and she groaned softly. That would be her mother.

Sighing, she made her way to the front door and jerked it open. "I know you're better at all this than me, but I know what I w-want..."

She stuttered into silence.

It wasn't her mother. It was Trip. Not a photograph in a magazine or a memory but the man himself. Lean, muscular, shockingly beautiful. And even as she registered the inappropriateness of those thoughts, given that he was supposed to be dead, he leaned into the door frame, one thick, dark eyebrow arched upward, his astonishing mouth curved into a shape that sent her stomach somersaulting.

"Good to know," he said in that familiar, deep transatlantic drawl. "Because so do I."

The Diamond Club

Billion-dollar secrets behind every door...

Welcome to The Diamond Club: the world's most exclusive society, open only to the ten richest men and women alive. The suites are opulent. The service is flawless. And privacy is paramount! You'll never see the details of these billionaires' blistering romances in any of the papers—but you can read all about them right here!

Baby Worth Billions by Lynne Graham

Pregnant Princess Bride by Caitlin Crews

Greek's Forbidden Temptation by Millie Adams

Italian's Stolen Wife by Lorraine Hall

Heir Ultimatum by Michelle Smart

His Runaway Royal by Clare Connelly

Reclaimed with a Ring by Louise Fuller

Stranded and Seduced by Emmy Grayson

All available now!

RECLAIMED WITH A RING

LOUISE FULLER

PRESENTS

Harlequin®
PRESENTS™

ISBN-13: 978-1-335-93904-3

Reclaimed with a Ring

Recycling programs for this product may not exist in your area.

 Harlequin Enterprises ULC
22 Adelaide St. West, 41st Floor
Toronto, Ontario M5H 4E3, Canada
www.Harlequin.com

Printed in Lithuania

MIX
Paper | Supporting responsible forestry
FSC® C021394

Louise Fuller was a tomboy who hated pink and always wanted to be the prince—not the princess! Now she enjoys creating heroines who aren't pretty pushovers but are strong, believable women. Before writing for Harlequin, she studied literature and philosophy at university, then worked as a reporter on her local newspaper. She lives in Royal Tunbridge Wells with her impossibly handsome husband, Patrick, and their six children.

Books by Louise Fuller

Harlequin Presents

Beauty in the Billionaire's Bed
The Italian's Runaway Cinderella
Maid for the Greek's Ring
Their Dubai Marriage Makeover
Returning for His Ruthless Revenge
Her Diamond Deal with the CEO

Christmas with a Billionaire

The Christmas She Married the Playboy

Hot Winter Escapes

One Forbidden Night in Paradise

Behind the Billionaire's Doors...

Undone in the Billionaire's Castle

Visit the Author Profile page
at Harlequin.com for more titles.

CHAPTER ONE

DESPITE THE HEAT and the humidity there was a crowd of maybe fifty or sixty photographers waiting.

But not for him.

Trip Winslow tilted his face towards the tinted window of the limousine.

Nobody knew that he was coming. Incredibly, and despite the plethora of communication platforms available in the modern world, he had managed to stay incognito. All thanks to a phone call to Lazlo, the manager of the Diamond Club. It was Lazlo who had arranged the hot bath, wet shave, private jet, car and driver and security detail swiftly, quietly and with the same unshakeable calm that he did everything. It was what made him invaluable to the ten richest people in the world who made up the small, elite membership of the club.

But Trip's disappearance was still the story of the hour, the year, maybe even the decade. After all, how many times did one of the wealthiest people on the planet just vanish into thin air?

So he'd anticipated that the paparazzi and news teams would be here in New York. His blue gaze moved assessingly over the huddle of mostly men prowling the steps up to the iconic gleaming glass and steel Winslow Building.

And yet it still felt like an ambush.

A ripple of panic skimmed over his skin, and for a moment he was back in the jungle, his heart pounding as he watched different men inch towards where he was pressed against a tree, their eyes narrowed, guns high against their chests like in the video games he had played incessantly as a teenager.

Only these gunmen were real. So were their bullets.

'Do you want me to go round the back, Mr Winslow? Or I can call Security. Get an extra team out to block off the road.'

For a fraction of a second, he didn't respond to the driver's question, not least because even now, ten months after his father's death, he was still struggling to remember that he was 'that' Mr Winslow. For him, the title would always belong to his father, Henry Winslow II. Of course, Trip's older brother, Charlie, wouldn't have given it a second thought.

His shoulders stiffened. In many ways, he'd felt as though he hardly knew his brother. And now he never would because Charlie was dead. Killed three years ago in a plane crash along with their mother.

Which left Trip.

The spare. The runner-up who had won by default.

Not that he hadn't proven himself worthy of being CEO. But Charlie had always been destined to take over the business. Partly because he was twelve years older, but also because their father had raised him from birth to be his heir so that he looked and acted the part.

Most important of all, Charlie was the type to defer to their father.

Unlike Trip.

He had been at odds with Henry Winslow II as far back as he could remember. Which probably explained why he had ended up being called Trip. That way, at least, his father could distance himself from the stubborn son who shared his name but rarely his opinions.

He glanced up, his gaze moving past the driver's inquiring eyes to meet his own in the rear-view mirror. They were the exact same blue as his father's. The only thing they had in common.

Like Charlie, his father was academically consistent, focused, disciplined, whereas he had oscillated between boredom and brilliance.

He had got into Harvard, like his father and Charlie, but had dropped out to set up a business that had failed in its first year. He'd learned from his mistakes though and his second venture was widely touted as a unicorn by the business media, reaching a billion-dollar valuation in its first year.

He had kept his stake and would probably have set up another business if his success hadn't caught the eye of his father. To his astonishment, Henry had reached out to him, invited him to take over the Far East division in Hong Kong.

His father hadn't gambled, had been notoriously risk averse, so Trip had known that he was being tested and that knowledge had given him a sense of purpose. He had effortlessly arrowed in on the failing areas of the

business and each of those sectors had then outperformed themselves under his leadership.

His father had grudgingly admitted that he had done
well, and, shortly before Charlie's death, Trip had been
allowed to go to London to head up the European division. There, his strokes of creative genius had attracted
the attention of the business press and given Winslow
Inc its most profitable year on record. But it had never
been enough as far as his father was concerned.

Because mistakes, failures, missteps had been unac-
ceptable to Henry Winslow II. A decorated naval officer who had taken over his father's modest construction
firm and turned it into the multinational conglomerate
it was today. A private, committed family man whose
one act of impulsiveness had led to a forty-two-year-long
marriage that had ended only by his wife's tragic death.

Trip gritted his teeth. Except it turned out his father
hadn't been that committed after all.

His spine tensed as he replayed the moment when
he'd found the letters among his father's things. Letters
from a woman named Kerry. Letters filled with unfiltered declarations of need and passion.

*I am blind without you...being with you will restore
my sight, my love...*

The shock had sent Trip spinning off course to Ecuador, to the churning white waters of the Rio Upano,
and from there into the rainforest and imprisonment at
the hands of a passing drugs cartel.

He stared through the window, his gaze snagging on
a couple weaving between the stationary cars. The tall
grey-haired man was holding the hand of the woman

beside him. His wife? Before Ecuador he would have made this assumption unthinkingly. Now, though, he could see only other possibilities.

His fingers clutched the upholstered armrest. Behind closed doors there had always been a distance between his parents so in some ways his father's infidelity should not have been that much of a surprise. But Henry Winslow II had led a note-perfect life, famously intolerant and unforgiving of failure in others, particularly in his youngest son. And yet, all along, he had been breaking the rules, lying, cheating, deceiving...

Was it any surprise Trip's world had tilted on its axis when he'd found out the truth?

'Mr Winslow?'

The driver's voice bumped into his thoughts and he dragged his gaze back to the photographers. Like all paparazzi, they looked hungry and determined. 'Let's go in the front.' He gestured to the car gliding to a halt in front of them. 'Security can handle them.'

It was the opposite of what his father would have done. Or maybe it wasn't. Having read those letters from his father's mistress, he wasn't sure he even knew who Henry Winslow II was any more.

As the driver opened the door, the heat hit him like a wall but he barely had time to register it before the photographers turned and saw him.

Their mouths collectively dropped open and there was a tiny suspension of air and noise as if the whole city were taken aback by his sudden appearance.

But then, it wasn't often someone came back from the dead.

'It's him,' he heard someone shout. 'It's Trip!'

And then, like fire ants sensing a juicy meal, they began swarming towards the car.

'Mr Winslow, is it true you were shot?'

'Did you lose your memory, Trip?'

'Were you hiding or lost?'

'Over here, over here, Mr Winslow—'

He was used to press attention, had grown up playing hide and seek with the paparazzi, but as the voice recorders and cameras rose like a wave he felt his heartbeat accelerate.

But the security detail was good and they held back the heaving, baying pack so he could make his way up the flight of steps into the office.

It was part of his father's world-conquering ethos that nature didn't intrude on the day-to-day running of his business. It didn't matter if New York was melting or buried under three feet of snow, the building was always the same unobtrusive, ambient temperature. And yet today the gleaming marble and wood panelled foyer felt somehow different. Cooler, familiar and yet altered in a way he couldn't quite put his finger on.

He felt different too. Which was no doubt why everyone was looking at him as if they'd seen a ghost. But then in a way they had.

'Mr Winslow.' The receptionist—Carole? Was that her name?—got to her feet, her eyes wide and stunned. Her colleague simply stared at him, slack-jawed.

'You're back. You're here—' Carole was blinking at him as if she had malfunctioned.

'Yes, I am.' He gave her a quick, dazzling smile that

snapped off as he jerked his head towards the ceiling.
'Are they in?'

By 'they', he meant the C-suite and it was a rhetori-
cal question. They were paid to be here, to manage the
ship while he was away, so where else would they be?

'Yes, Mr Mason is holding an extraordinary meeting
of the board this morning.'

'Good. Then let me go make sure it really is *extra*ordinary.'

He felt rather than saw her reach for the phone as he
walked towards the lifts. But that was okay. It would
give them time to roll out the red carpet. Hail, the con-
quering hero, he thought, stepping into the elevator.

As it rose upwards, he shivered. Was it him, or was
the air in the building growing colder the higher they
went? But that question stayed unanswered as the lift
doors opened and Mason Cooper, Winslow's CFO and
Trip's godfather, strode towards him, arms outstretched.

'Trip—'

He grunted as the older man pulled him into a bear
hug. Mason was a firm believer in tough love and over
the years he had often taken an unwilling Trip aside
for pep talks. Trip felt a sudden urge to lean into the
older man.

'I don't understand.' Mason was patting his shoulders and arms as if to prove to himself that Trip was not
a figment of his imagination. 'How did you get here?
How are you? What happened? Where have you been?'

'I can fill you in another time.' He clapped Mason
on the back to stop the spate of questions that he had no
intention of answering. 'It's a long and convoluted story

and right now I just want things to get back to normal.'
The trouble was he no longer knew what that was, Trip
thought, his gaze snagging on his father's portrait as
they walked past the boardroom.

'Of course you do.' Mason nodded. 'Let's go to your
office.'

'It's okay, I know the way,' he said irritably as his
CFO put a hand on his shoulder to guide him. 'I wasn't
away that long.'

Mason lifted an eyebrow. 'I'd say five weeks alone in
an Ecuadorian jungle is quite long enough.'

It had felt like five years, Trip thought. In places,
the canopy of leaves had been so dense that night and
day had often felt interchangeable, never-ending and
he would have to stop moving or risk tripping over the
treacherous, twisting branches and invisible dips in the
forest floor. And always there had been that pattering
sound of water, dripping against the vegetation.

But that had been only a part of it. Some of the time,
he would probably never know exactly how long for certain, there had been simply the absolute darkness of the
blindfold and the ropes biting into his wrists.

He had never felt so alone, so helpless, not even when
he was a child, and it started to become obvious to him
that he experienced the world in a different way from
the rest of his family.

But it was not in his nature to show weakness or re-
veal vulnerability, particularly here. Here, he was the
boss, the man in charge. He was not just Mr Winslow,
he was *the* Mr Winslow, and, now that he was back, he

was going to make sure that that name was associated with him for ever, and not with his grandfather or father.

As he dropped down into the seat behind his desk, there was a knock at the door and Conrad Stiles, the chief operating officer, and Ron Maidman, the head of marketing, walked into the office, their feet faltering, faces freezing into masks of shock and disbelief as they saw him. He wasn't as close to them as he was Mason but they both shook his hand and clapped him on the shoulder.

'I can't believe you're really here.' Maidman was shaking his head. 'I thought I was hallucinating. What happened out there? Are you okay? Are you hurt?'

'Another time, Ron. Like I said to Mason, I just want to get back behind the wheel, so why don't you take a seat and talk me through what's been happening?'

Was it his imagination or did all their faces stiffen?

Mason nodded. 'Of course, of course. Obviously, in your absence, we had to make some decisions.'

Trip stared across the desk at the three men sitting opposite him. 'I'm sure you took care of everything,' he said softly. He couldn't quite keep the edge of bitterness out of his voice. His father might have formally named him his successor, but he'd made it clear that he expected his son to draw on the experience and expertise of his C-suite.

He'd been grateful for their advice and support in the immediate aftermath of his father's death, but things were different now. Okay, he'd been a little off his game at the start, but he'd been running the business for ten months without a hiccup.

'Now I'm back, and, in light of recent events, I want to make a few changes. You see, I had a lot of time to think in the jungle and I have a few ideas that I want to set in motion.'

Mason nodded. 'And obviously we will be more than happy to discuss that but right now you should be at home, resting. You've had a traumatic experience—'

'The doctor said I was fine, and I am,' he said impatiently. There was a bluebottle crashing against the glass, buzzing around the edges of the window frame as it tried to find an opening, and for a moment he stared at it, body tensing as he remembered his own equally frantic attempts to push through the towering vegetation.

'I don't want to rest. What I need is to get back to work.'

Conrad cleared his throat. 'And you will, but, as you pointed out, we need to bring you up to speed first. Clarify a few things. In light of recent events,' he added, his eyes meeting Trip's.

'Meaning?' Trip lounged back in his chair, trying to slow his heartbeat. The script he'd prepared in his head in the car was already starting to unravel.

'Trip—you've been missing for weeks. We didn't know where you were, if you were even alive—'

'You make it sound as though I planned for that to happen.' His eyes narrowed. 'I can promise you I didn't. I certainly didn't expect to cross paths with a cartel. Or be taken prisoner.'

'Is that what happened?' Mason looked shocked. 'My God, Trip, I don't know what to say—'

Trip gazed past him at the heat-soaked city skyline.

That was just the start of it. But he didn't want to think about what followed. Not here, not now, not in front of these men. His breath caught in his chest. Not when he didn't know how he would react.

'Did they hurt you?'

'I'm fine.'

He stretched out his legs and pressed his spine against the leather upholstery. It wasn't a complete lie. He had been seen by a doctor in Ecuador shortly after he'd stumbled out of the jungle and, aside from a couple of nasty cuts and a mild case of dehydration, he was physically fine.

But he was sleeping badly, waking in darkness and sweat, cold with a fear that he could only shift by opening his eyes and getting out of bed so that he could feel the carpet beneath his feet. Because that was the only way he could convince himself that he had been dreaming.

'I'm glad to hear it.' Ron hesitated. 'We all are, obviously—' he gave Trip a nervous smile '—and we did everything we could to help find you from this end, but part of the problem was that we didn't know where you were.'

Trip frowned. 'I don't need permission to take a vacation, Ron. I'm the CEO.'

His head of marketing flushed and there was a small pause as the three older men glanced furtively at one another. 'Not permission, no, but it would have been helpful to know where you were,' Mason said after a moment.

Conrad frowned. 'We thought you were dead.'

Trip stared at him steadily, a ghost of a smile playing around his hard mouth. 'Sorry to disappoint.'

Mason shook his head. 'That's not fair, Trip—'

'No, what's not fair is you guys giving me a hard time for something that was out of my control. But it's in the past now and I'm here, so no harm, no foul.'

He was done explaining himself.

'No harm.' Mason was staring at him as if he'd grown an extra head. 'You were a prisoner of a drug cartel!'

'And I got away. Without a scratch.' That was true… ish but any detail would only serve to undermine his argument.

'And we're pleased to hear that.' Ron frowned. 'Unfortunately the business wasn't so lucky. The share prices plummeted—'

'I heard,' he cut across the older man. 'And now they've gone back up. Gone higher, in fact.'

Mason was shaking his head. 'That's not how your father did business. It's not how we do business.'

'There is no we,' he said coldly. 'This is *my* business. I'm the CEO.'

'But that can only stay true if you are the best person for the job,' Mason said, his eyes finding Trip's. 'The position of CEO is not allocated simply on the basis of surname or bloodline.'

'Is that right?' Trip said softly.

There was a long, pulsing silence. Finally, Mason cleared his throat. 'Look, Trip. Your father wanted you to take over the business, but he also gave us the option to intervene at our discretion.'

Yes, because he had never truly considered his youngest son as anything other than a spare, Trip thought, letting his gaze move across the distant skyline. He was too impulsive, too headstrong ever to see eye to eye with his father, but after Charlie's death Henry had had no alternative but to leave him the company.

Suddenly and fiercely, Trip wanted all three of them out of his office.

'You can't fire me.'

Mason gave him a small, stiff smile. 'You're not being fired, Trip. But we answer to the shareholders. As do you.'

Pushing back from his desk, Trip stood. 'Exactly, and in case you've forgotten I'm not just the CEO, I'm the majority shareholder.'

'Yes, you are.' The older man nodded. 'But as was explained to you when you took over, some of those shares are held in a trust of which we are the trustees. We have the power to use those shares to remove any CEO temporarily or permanently whose actions are damaging to the interests of the shareholders. And what happened in Ecuador…what could have happened…has raised issues. Shareholders like stability.'

Trip held his gaze. 'I do things my way. If they don't like it—'

'They don't, Trip. That's the point. They want to see that you are serious about running the business and, I'm afraid, currently your behaviour is not speaking to that.'

'My behaviour—?'

He felt a rush of fury. What about his father's behaviour? Had anyone held him to account for having a long-term mistress? As his eyes flicked across the other men's faces, he felt a slithering panic weave through his chest. Had his father confided in them? Did they know who Kerry was? But he couldn't bring himself to ask. To ask the question would give the relationship a validity it didn't deserve.

'They—*we*—need a CEO who is stable and mature and focused.'

'I am all of those things— What?' The three men were shaking their heads. He gritted his teeth.

Mason sighed. 'You have the makings of a great business leader but you are impulsive, reckless even. Look at how you just went off to Ecuador on a whim—'

Not a whim, he thought, his chest clamping tight so that it was suddenly hard to breathe. It had been an imperative. He had felt as if he were suffocating in New York, smothered by the weight of his father's hypocrisy.

'And your private life is chaotic. Your friends make headlines for all the wrong reasons. Maybe if you had a steady girlfriend to anchor you…but according to the Internet you spend your free time running around the city bedding every woman you meet.'

His eyes narrowed. 'I'm not running around the city bedding every woman I meet. As a matter of fact, I'm engaged.'

The words were out of his mouth before he'd even realised what he was about to say and a stunned, fascinated silence spread across the room, blanketing all other sound. The other men looked, if anything, more shocked than before. As if it was easier to believe he had come back from the dead than that he was engaged.

Ron Maidman recovered first. '*Engaged!* To whom?'

Trip blinked. *Good question*, he thought.

Marriage had always been one of those things he thought about in an abstract way. It felt inevitable, in that most people tried it once so he imagined he would too. But the path there was hazy and uncharted. And besides, he had no real understanding of what marriage meant. His parents were often held up as an example of a happy, devoted couple, but that was just the public facade. In private their relationship had been more two people coexisting than sharing lives.

He felt the tractor-beam force of the other men's combined gaze and, setting his face back to blank, he reached for the name of the most stable, mature, focused woman he could think of. A name that would shut down his tormentors and give him back the upper hand.

'To Lily. Lily Dempsey.'

Now the astonishment in the room rose to such almost comic levels that he would have laughed. Except he didn't feel like laughing.

Lily Dempsey. With her Mona Lisa smile and cool, dismissive grey eyes.

She was the dictionary definition of stable, mature and focused. Pretty much an 'anchor' in human form.

Unfortunately, she also hated him.

To be fair, he wasn't her biggest fan either. Not for any specific reason. They just always seemed to clash, although that only happened when she acknowledged his existence. Often she seemed to look straight through him. And that was such a unique and uniquely irritating experience that he had found himself deliberately crossing her path, only to regret it when she spoke to him in the cool, withering tone that made it clear she found his charms skin-deep.

Which made the fact that they had been secretly sleeping together in the two months before he had gone to Ecuador not just incomprehensible but a mystery that was unsolvable.

It was just sex, of course. He'd never planned on taking it any further than that one night, but then they had bumped into one another at another charity event and it had been just the same. And it had kept happening and suddenly it had been happening for a month, then another.

And he still didn't understand why.

The phrase chalk and cheese could have been invented for them, but in bed they were like flames merging and curling around one another. His body tensed, groin hardening so that he had to blank his mind to the memory of her body wrapped around his.

'You're engaged to Lily Dempsey?'

He stared across the room at Mason's frowning face. No, he thought.

'Yes,' he lied. 'We've been seeing each other for a couple of months, but she wanted to keep it on the down-low because of her father.'

That at least was true. Lily had been insistent that they keep the relationship quiet, presumably because she didn't want to cause any distracting noise around her father's career as a senator, and Trip hadn't cared one way or the other. There were very few people whose opinion mattered to him. Nor did he feel the need to explain himself to anyone.

Which was lucky, because he couldn't rationalise his attraction to Lily. It didn't make sense. They didn't make sense.

Which was why he'd ended things. Except that wasn't true either. The reason he'd ended it was because of those damned letters.

Reading through, he'd felt conned, duped, betrayed, and he'd wanted to smash things. In that moment, there had been just too much overlap between the passion and secrecy of his father's affair and his heated, clandestine encounters with Lily, and he'd been angry and she'd been there and something had snapped inside him.

Ron got to his feet. 'Congratulations, Trip. That's wonderful news.'

He held out his hand, and Trip shook it mechanically.

'I'm so pleased for you,' Mason said quietly. 'Lily is a wonderful woman, and I know how much your father enjoyed working with her.'

'Congratulations.' Conrad joined the other two smiling men to take Trip's hand. 'But what are you doing here?' His smile stiffened. 'She does know you're back?'

No, not yet, he thought. Nor did she know they were engaged, but that wouldn't be a problem.

Would it?

He had a sudden, sharp flashback to their last meeting at her apartment. He hadn't quite known how she would react but, true to form, she had confounded him. 'It was just a fling,' she'd said. She wouldn't pine away if he never came back.

For some reason, ego probably, her words had stung more than they should, enough to echo inside his head during the weeks of his incarceration. Now he had to hope she would be so swept away by his sudden reappearance that she would be willing to agree to anything. After all, what woman wouldn't want to marry one of the ten richest men on the planet?

'Yes, of course. But she wanted me to come in, in person, to reassure you,' he said quickly, lying again.

'Which is why she's such an excellent choice.' Mason glanced over at the other two men, clearly pleased. 'But you've been through so much, Trip. What you need is some time and space to process everything that's happened and the best person to help you do that is Lily. You should be with her.'

He nodded slowly. 'You're right. I should. In fact, I might just head off there now.'

Not to process what had happened, he thought as he stalked past yet more astonished employees back towards the elevator. But because he needed to catch Lily and convince her to be his fiancée before she heard about their supposed engagement from a third party and blew the whole thing apart.

'So are you thinking a Kingston or an Empire swag?'

Gazing at the swatches of fabric, Lily Jane Dempsey frowned. She had no idea what she was thinking. Her current curtains were perfectly fine. Perfect, in fact, she thought, glancing over at the draping folds of cream silk. So why was she bothering to change them? Why was she here, talking about swag options with her mother's interior designer, Samantha?

Her hand moved to her throat, to the pulse beating

against the smooth skin like a moth trapped in a jar, feeling, not her fingers, but his mouth.

Trip's mouth.

The same mouth that had kissed her to the edge of reason as she'd arched beneath him in the bedroom upstairs, and then told her that he was going to Ecuador.

He was the reason she had decided to change her curtains.

Because she couldn't change the past, couldn't take back the last words she'd spoken to him, and she had needed something to take her mind off the fact that he was gone and that she was partly responsible because she had told him to get out of her sight, to go to Ecuador and not come back.

And he hadn't. He had disappeared into the rainforest and, despite the various search teams that had been sent to look for him, he hadn't been found, and after five weeks he was not just missing but presumed dead.

Only it wasn't just guilt she felt. Part of her hated him for disappearing like that. Sometimes her fury made it impossible to sleep and then she would pace the apartment, imagining his return and feeling almost giddy with relief that he was alive.

Her hands clenched. But only because she would have a chance to kill him or at least slap his handsome face for being such a selfish, thoughtless idiot. Because that hurt—to think that she would never see those glittering blue eyes again. And when she thought about that, about a world where Trip didn't exist, she had to distract herself with work or by helping her mother on her various committees. Or by changing her curtains.

But it was hard to distract herself, because she had known Trip her whole life. They had grown up in the same social circles. Their parents had been on first-name terms.

Their relationship had been a little more frosty.

Or it had been when he'd actually noticed that she was there. Which he hadn't very often because he was all blue eyes and smooth golden skin and tawny-coloured hair falling across his forehead, and that smile, whereas she—

Her eyes moved to the mirror above the fireplace and she felt the familiar twinge of disappointment.

She'd often wondered why her parents had chosen to call her Lily first and Jane second. Lily conjured up flawless creamy petals and a seductive scent and she was neither flawless nor seductive. She was plain, like her middle name.

It wasn't a humblebrag. It was just the facts. Her hair was mousey and frizzy—although she had learned how to tame it now—her eyes were grey and she had a small bump on her nose that was absent from both her patrician-faced parents. Body wise, she was slim and her legs were long. Too long. Long enough to earn the nickname 'daddy-long-legs'.

She didn't light up a room as Trip did. Mostly she was invisible.

Then suddenly three months ago, without warning, without understanding why, they had ended up in bed. And it had been intoxicating and terrifying in equal measure, not least because it was pure happenstance.

If his father, Henry, hadn't set up the Alessandra

Winslow Endowment for Music in memory of his wife, they might have simply remained as occasional sparring partners. But after Henry's death, Trip had reluctantly taken his father's place and suddenly he was there in her life, pulsing with heat and energy like a meteorite, lighting up the world, trailing a promise of something that she had never allowed herself to imagine because it didn't happen to women who looked like her.

She had let down her guard.

And there was no excuse. Not after what had happened the last time with Cameron, when her neediness and longing to be liked had blinded her to what was hiding in plain sight and ultimately put her brother in harm's way.

Then again, she was only human, and Trip Winslow was the most beautiful man she had ever known. In a crowded room and at a distance, the flawless symmetry of his features and blatant masculinity made him conspicuous. But up close his beauty was astonishing, mesmerising.

Nothing could have prepared her for how it felt to sit opposite him and just gaze and gaze. And every time his gaze had met hers, it had felt like a caress. And that had shocked her, scared her, angered her. How could you be so attracted to someone when you disliked them so much? It defied the laws of attraction.

Feeling Samantha's gaze on her face, she realised that she had no idea how much time had passed since the woman had asked her about her curtains, or how to reply.

'The Kingston,' she said quickly.

'I was hoping you'd say that.' Samantha gave her an approving smile. 'This room demands drama and a Kingston always adds that little va-va-voom. And what about the colour? Are you sure about switching from the blue to the green?' she asked casually.

Lily gritted her teeth. Her mother loved neutrals, but Lily had wanted a change from creams and whites, and blue, the right, flattering, timeless shade of blue, was Laura's compromise. But Lily liked the green and, for once, she was going to put her foot down.

'Absolutely,' she said firmly.

There was a quivering silence as Samantha held her gaze a moment too long and then the designer smiled stiffly and glanced down at her tablet. 'Now, I know we haven't discussed the bathroom blinds, but your mother did ask me to take a quick peek—'

It was another hour before Samantha left.

Flopping down on the sofa in a way that would have made her mother wince, Lily picked up one of the magazines from the coffee table and opened it at a random page, and then wished she hadn't as she glanced down to find Trip's out-of-this-world face staring up at her.

She felt a spasm of pain around her heart.

It had been weeks now since he'd gone missing. Five weeks and three days. There had been a lot of supposition about what had happened in Ecuador, but few facts had emerged from the rainforest. The one that had stuck in her mind was the discovery of the Jeep he'd been driving. Watching the news, she had stared at the bullet holes in the bonnet and doors, feeling devastated, then angry, then stricken with guilt.

The buzzer to her door sounded and she groaned softly. That would be her mother.

Laura Dempsey had been in charge of the original decor of the flat and Lily had fully expected her to be in charge of this revamp, but then her mother had called to say she had double-booked.

Lily had been slightly relieved, then felt guilty for feeling that way. Now she wondered why, because of course her mother would have 'asked' Samantha to call her the moment she left the apartment. No doubt the designer had let slip that Lily had chosen the green drapes, not the blue, and so here was Laura all ready to right the wrong—

Sighing, she made her way to the front door and jerked it open. 'I know you're better at all this than me, but I know what I w-want—'

She stuttered into silence. For a moment the apartment behind her seemed to fold in on itself as if some vast, invisible explosion had happened.

It wasn't her mother. It was Trip. Lean, muscular and as shockingly beautiful as ever, he leaned against the door frame, one thick, dark eyebrow arched, his astonishing mouth curved into a shape that made her heart relocate to her throat.

'Good to know,' he said in that familiar, deep Transatlantic drawl. 'Because so do I.'

CHAPTER TWO

LILY COULDN'T MOVE. She wanted to, but she felt winded and dizzy.

He was alive. *He was alive.*

She lifted her hand, wanting, needing to touch him, to prove that he was real, then pressed it against her throat, to where her pulse was pounding out of time.

'How? When?' Her voice was barely a breath. 'I thought you were—' Lost. Dead. Gone for ever. She couldn't say the words out loud.

He shrugged. 'Let's just say I got unavoidably delayed.'

When she didn't respond, his forehead creased infinitesimally and he fished out his phone and swiped across the screen.

She stared down at the picture. Trip was striding up the steps in front of the Winslow Building just as if it were any other day. Words jumped out at her from the accompanying story. Captive. Cartel. Escape.

Her mind was a bumper car, jolting back and forth and side to side as questions slammed into each other. 'Is this true?' she managed finally.

'It's a version of the truth. The kind that sells papers.'

It was too much, him being here. The force of him, being so alive and real, his body filling the doorway, broad-chested and taller than in her memory, those arresting blue eyes and lips that she knew could send ripples of heat rolling through her like wildfire. The shock of him and the chaotic emotions provoked by his presence filled her head, her chest. That was why she couldn't breathe, she told herself. Why her body felt as if it were coming apart at the seams, why she felt as if it belonged to someone else.

'Why are you here?' she said hoarsely.

'I wanted to see you. To let you know that I was back, in person. I didn't want you to hear it from the news.'

'Well, now I've heard—' Relief and other nameless feelings she couldn't, wouldn't acknowledge were swept away by an anger she had never felt before and she tried to shut the door but he wedged his foot in it as they did in old black and white films.

'What are you doing?' she snapped.

'We need to talk.'

'By "we" you mean you, because I have nothing to say to you.' She frowned. 'Oh, actually, yes, I do. It's goodbye.'

She pushed against the door, but he held it open easily.

'I'm happy to do the talking. Come on, Lily. I've just come back from the dead.' The curl to his mouth made her feel off balance. 'Surely you can give me five minutes.'

'Fine. You have five minutes and then you will leave.'

She let go of the door and he shrugged away from the frame and strolled past her.

Her breath was running wild in her chest.

Her eyes glanced over his superbly tailored and no doubt paralyzingly expensive dark suit and white shirt, over the scratches and his slightly too long hair that gave him the untamed air of a Hollywood action hero.

The stupidity of their mismatched relationship made her stomach clench.

'I must say you don't seem very pleased to see me,' he said, stopping in the middle of the sitting room and turning to face her.

Her heart lurched. Pleased didn't exactly cover the vortex of emotions churning inside her.

'I'm glad you're safe.' She spoke to a point slightly above his left shoulder but her peripheral vision was greedily filling in the details so that she knew he was staring at her with those intensely blue eyes, and that his glossy brown hair was falling across his face.

'That's it?' He moved towards her and she had to dig her heels into the cream carpet to stop herself from stepping backwards. 'It's a little underwhelming, wouldn't you say?'

There was a mocking note in his voice and quite suddenly she was furious again. How could he joke about any of this?

'What were you expecting? A ticker-tape parade?' She spoke briskly. Oh, why had she agreed to let him in? She had prayed for him to be alive but now that he was, now that he was here, it was making her head spin.

'The mayor called on my way over here and offered,

but I said no,' he said in that casual drawl that tugged at each of her nerve endings separately. 'I didn't want any fuss made. Not from him, anyway. But you…' He paused, his eyes locking with hers. 'I was hoping you might be a little more *expressive*. I mean, we were going out—'

It was a trick, a hook, and he was taunting her to take the bait. She knew that and yet she still couldn't stop her head from snapping round.

'We never went out.'

His eyes were clear and intensely blue. 'No, you're right. We always stayed in.'

The trap slammed shut. A prickling heat skated across her skin and she felt her body tighten. Everywhere. Her heart was pounding as if she were running hard, and that was what she should be doing. Running as fast and as far as she could from this beautiful, dangerous man.

He made her want things, and she knew all too well how wanting could make you lose sight of what mattered. She had done so before with Cameron and there had been horrific, far-reaching consequences. But it had been different with Trip. They weren't friends. They hadn't talked or gone out on dates. There had been no promises made, no expectations, and she had liked that he wasn't hers to lose. The fact that they had been using each other for sex was a kind of equality she'd found thrilling in some way.

And yet it had hurt more than it should when he'd ended things. And now that he was here, standing in front of her, it hurt to look at him, to remember what they'd had.

'To be honest what happened between us was so brief it kind of slipped my mind,' she said coolly.

He paused, just for a second. 'Then maybe it's time I jogged your memory.'

She felt suddenly unsteady on her feet, like a boxer on the ropes. Pressing her nails into her palms, she forced herself to hold his gaze. 'I'm not a fan of retrospectives. Personally, I find it better to live in the present.'

He was facing the window and in the sunlight through the glass his pupils were almost invisible, so that she felt as though she were drowning in the blue of his irises.

'I couldn't agree more,' he said softly. 'So here I am, ready to engage.'

She stared at him in confusion and felt a shiver of apprehension ripple down her spine. 'With what? You came to tell me you were back, and you have, so what else is there?'

'I told you. I want to talk.' There was a split second of silence, and then he said softly, 'About you and me. About us.'

The word reverberated around the room as she shook her head. 'There is no us.' There were just darkness and bodies and warm breath and damp skin.

The sudden force of her heartbeat made her reach out and grip the back of an armchair.

'Not currently,' he said after a moment. 'But there could be. I want there to be.'

The bluntness of that statement made her feel hot inside, scalded almost. She felt her face grow warm and she knew that she was blushing.

'And why would you want that?' she said stiffly, hating him, but hating herself more for the shiver that ran over her skin.

He stared down at her, that mouth of his curving up. 'Because we have a connection.'

That was one word for it. For a moment she saw herself on the bed upstairs, breathless with wanting him, arms stretched out above her head, wrists in his hand, her body arching to meet his, tilting her hips up, driving herself against him. And his face above her, eyes dark and bright with a heat that seemed to pour straight into her.

'You're unbelievable.' She took an unsteady step backwards, anger blotting out the memory of their 'connection'. 'Seriously? Did you come all the way over here because you thought I might have sex with you? Because that isn't going to happen.' It shouldn't have happened before.

She knew it then. Knew that she was playing with fire. Although truthfully it had felt more as if she were dancing around the mouth of an active volcano, because even when he wasn't the focus of an international search and rescue, Trip made headlines. All those weeks playing hide and seek with the paparazzi had been part of the thrill of it, but if anyone had caught them, then what?

She shivered. And it would all be so much worse now.

Shaking her head, she met his gaze. 'Look, what we had worked for a few months, but it ended and frankly I'm done sneaking around like some grounded teenager. Next time I decide to see someone it will be out in the open, public. Real.'

'Real?' He frowned. 'You mean love?'

Did she? Like most people, she hoped love might happen one day. That someone would love and cherish and honour her. But given that the only time she'd imagined herself in love, she had been humiliated and deceived and made to feel like a fool, it was more an ideal right now than a likelihood.

It certainly wasn't going to happen with Trip. There were just too many differences between them. She had ignored that with Cameron and her brother was still paying the price.

Once bitten, twice shy.

Not bitten…mauled, she thought, throat tightening as she heard Cameron's voice. *Why would any man settle for you?*

Blanking her mind, she lifted her chin. 'Yes, I suppose so.'

Unsurprisingly Trip looked baffled, but then it seemed unlikely that love, the true, everlasting kind, the sort that involved promises to be kept and commitments to be honoured, the 'growing old and sick together' variety, came high on his agenda.

'Or something like it.' She felt suddenly self-conscious. Why was she even talking about love with Trip Winslow? This was a man who had turned up on her doorstep hoping for an afternoon of sex without strings.

'Something like it,' he repeated slowly. 'And what would it look like, that something?'

'I don't know.' She glared at him. 'Does it matter?'

'It might. You see, in answer to your question, no, I didn't come all the way over here because I thought you might have sex with me.' He gave her a long, steady look, as if he was trying to see beneath her skin.

'I came here to ask you to marry me.'

If he'd asked her to fly to the moon with him, she couldn't have been more shocked. For a moment, she just stared at him, and then she gave a small, brittle laugh.

'You think I'm joking?' His eyes had narrowed.

'Yes, of course. Obviously.' Abruptly she sobered up. 'Although it's not a very funny joke.'

'It's not a joke at all. I want you to marry me.'

'Have you lost your mind?' She held up her hand as he opened his mouth to reply. 'You don't need to answer that. Clearly you have. Why else would you be asking me to be your wife?'

'Because I have a problem,' he said in that smooth way of his, all silk on the surface, but steel beneath. 'I want it to go away and I think you can help make that happen. Just in the short term.'

'By marrying you?' She met his gaze. 'Sorry to burst your bubble, but from where I'm standing that sounds more like a problem than a solution.'

For a moment he didn't answer. Instead, he leaned forward and picked up the swatch of blue silk that she'd been considering for the curtains.

'I like this colour,' he said softly. It was almost an exact match for his eyes, and she felt her face grow warm as he rubbed it between his fingers. Remembering the urgent press of his hands on her and the dark hunger in his eyes, she felt a sharp heat shoot through her and, terrified that he would see it on her face, she snatched the swatch from his hand.

'Well, I don't. I prefer the green, and stop pretend-ing you care about my curtains. Or me. All we did was have sex—'

'We did.' His gaze dropped to where she could feel her pulse beating in her throat.

Ignoring the shiver of something hot and liquid trem-bling across her skin, Lily glared at him. 'Sex isn't a reason to get married. Thank you, but no, I don't want to marry you.'

There was a short silence and then he turned towards her, and she felt a current of awareness spill over her skin. She was over him in every way it was possible to be over a man. Unfortunately, her body didn't appear to have received that memo.

'I need this.'

His voice sounded taut. There was anger there but frustration too, and pain. 'You see, Winslow is my busi-ness. It's my name above the door. I'm the majority shareholder, but some of my shares are held in a trust and if the trustees think that the actions of the CEO are incompatible with or detrimental to the effective run-ning of the business, then they can remove him or her.'

She gave a humourless laugh.

'You mean for some baffling reason they would have preferred that the man in charge hadn't got himself held prisoner by a drug cartel in an Ecuadorian rainforest?' She shook her head. 'How unreasonable of them.'

His gaze didn't flicker but she saw a dangerous glint in his blue eyes. 'I went to Ecuador to go white water rafting.'

A pulse of anger beat across her skin. 'On some of

the most dangerous rapids in the world, so you knew there was a possibility you might drown. You just hadn't factored in getting shot at or being held captive or getting lost in a rainforest.' She felt a stab of pain, imagining his beautiful eyes staring sightlessly up at the sky. How dared he risk his life for some stupid momentary thrill? Tears pricked behind her eyes, and she blinked them away, stonewalling the feeling as she watched his face harden.

'I don't have a death wish so, no, I wasn't thinking I might drown. I like the challenge, the purpose. There's a clarity in the moment—'

'In the moment?' She cut across him. 'And what about the aftermath? Everyone thought you were dead. Half the Ecuadorian police force was looking for you.'

He shrugged. 'It's their job.'

She raised an eyebrow. 'Yeah, I'm sure that's why they signed up for public service. To search for stupid "thrillionaires" who get themselves abducted.'

His eyes didn't leave hers as his jaw tightened, his expression hard and unforgiving and she saw the emotion smouldering there, the male pride and arrogance. 'I've already had one lecture this morning. I didn't come here for another.'

'That's a pity, because that's all you're getting from me,' she said crisply. 'But don't worry, I'm sure there are queues of women who will be more than willing to accept your proposal,' she said, keeping her eyes averted from the temptingly smooth, tanned skin of his arms. 'I don't even know why you asked me. You want a wife, and we barely managed a two-month one-night stand.'

His eyes rested on her face. 'I don't remember you complaining at the time. Moaning, gasping, crying out my name, sure…but not complaining.'

There was a hoarse softness in his voice that made her shiver, remembering the noises she'd made as she had come apart in his arms and against his mouth. It was suddenly difficult to breathe, much less speak.

She gritted her teeth. It wasn't fair of him to talk about the two of them in those moments. But then what did he know of fairness? He took his looks and charm, and wealth, for granted, assuming that they were his by right. He had never looked in the mirror and felt like an imposter or a let-down. Had never been surrounded by his peers and felt out of his depth.

Meeting his gaze, she shrugged. 'So I enjoyed having sex with you. That's all it was. I'm not going to take part in some charade of a marriage to get you out of a hole you dug yourself.'

He made a noise that was a mix of irritation and impatience. 'But it's not just my hole any more. It's our hole. Officially. In that it's in the open, public. Real. As far as they're concerned.'

They? The apprehension she had felt earlier was no longer a ripple but a huge, towering wave. 'Did you tell someone that you were going to come here and ask me to marry you?'

He shook his head.

'I didn't, no. It wouldn't have made sense. You see, I'd already told them we were engaged. That we were engaged before I left the States.' Now, he was shrugging off his jacket and rolling up his sleeves just like some husband in a sitcom.

'Look, believe me, I don't want to get married either, but I'm not going to lose my business over one holiday from hell. I need to look as if I'm changing. That's why I need a wife. The trustees my father appointed are his peers. They have his values. They see marriage as a stabilising influence. They were putting pressure on me and I needed a name. But it had to be to the right woman. You know, someone reliable, sensible, unadventurous.'

She lifted her chin. 'And you thought of me? How flattering.' Curling her fingers into her palms, she stared at him, humiliated that was the only reason he had chosen her. Did he think, because she wasn't some leggy model type with bee-stung lips, that she didn't have feelings?

'And it did the trick. You should have seen their faces light up. They like you, Lily.'

He had it all worked out, she thought, wishing she had never opened the door and let him back into her home, into her life.

'I'm sure they do. It's you that's the problem.' Taking a jagged breath, she shook her head. 'But you're not my problem.' He had never been her anything, nor did she want him to be. Twisting her wrist, she tapped her watch. 'And you've had your five minutes. So I suggest you call up your trustees and tell them you made a mistake. That you spoke rashly. I'm sure they'll have no trouble believing you. You can see yourself out, can't you?'

Spinning away from him, she walked over to the far

side of the room and flicked through one of the fabric books that Samantha had left behind. There was silence and she felt rather than saw him move. Her chest tightened with both relief and misery that he could find it so easy to walk away, but then he'd had practice.

She heard a rustling sound and, frowning, she turned and felt her stomach drop. Trip was lounging on the sofa, flicking through a magazine, his long legs stretched in front of him. Glancing up at her, he held it open.

'There was a good turnout that night, wasn't there? It's a nice photo too.'

For a moment she didn't respond, couldn't respond. She was too fazed by the picture. It had been taken the night of the auction when she had opened her tablet only to find that she hadn't uploaded her speech.

The same night that she and Trip had sex for the first time.

They were standing together, not touching, but she could remember how it had felt standing so close to him, his height, the curve of his muscles, the lightning snap of his eyes and that energy fizzing off his skin.

Her eyes fixed on the photograph. He looked like he always did. A masterclass in symmetry and flawless masculinity. Cool, confident, at ease with the cameras, whereas she…

Throat tightening, her gaze shifted to her own face.

She looked stiff and dazed. Partly because she was still reeling from the shock of Trip stepping up and giving a speech without any planning or preparation, but also because growing up with train-track braces had left her horribly self-conscious about smiling.

'It's just a photo.'

He was shaking his head. 'It's a story. The start of a fairy tale in New York.' His eyes on hers were as soft and intimate as a caress. 'A man and a woman who grew up in the same city, paths never quite crossing until, one day, fate pushes them together and they become lovers.'

Lovers. The word fizzed in her mouth and she felt heat break out on her skin. Trip wasn't the first man she'd had sex with, but he was her first lover.

Before him, she had understood the mechanics of sex and it had always been pleasant enough, only she hadn't been able to see why everyone made it into such a big deal.

Trip had made her see.

It had been revelatory. Sex with him had been wild, frantic. It had snatched her breath away. Left her reeling and hollowed out with a need she had never felt before. The more they'd touched and kissed and caressed, the more she'd wanted, and, like an addict, she'd lost touch with reality so that for the first time in her entire life she had felt beautiful, special.

But then he'd ended it.

Out of the blue. Just turned up, twitching with an anger she hadn't understood, still didn't understand, and he had ended it with her.

Folding her arms protectively in front of her body, she said coolly, 'Have you forgotten which way the door is?'

He let the magazine drop open onto the coffee table. 'Nice swerve, but I know you remember what we had. We could build on that.' His voice was a lazy drawl that played havoc with her nerve endings.

She gave him an icy glare. 'What I remember is you telling me that it had all gone on a little longer than you planned.' She could hear the bitterness in her voice, but she didn't care. All the pent-up confusion and anger and fear of the last few weeks seemed to have coalesced into one accusatory stream. 'What I remember is you standing in this room, itching to be gone.'

'And now I'm back.'

He got to his feet and she felt her body tense and soften at the same time as he walked towards her. She took a defensive step away from him, but he kept moving. Pressing the soles of her shoes into the rug, she held up a hand.

'Don't come any closer—'

'Because you don't trust yourself.' His teasing, dangerously sensuous mouth pulled into a smile that made her breath go shallow.

'Because you will regret it if you do,' she said stiffly.

The gleam in his eyes got more intense, and he took an infinitesimal step towards her.

'Why? Are you going to smother me with some swatches?'

He jerked the fabric in her hand and she should have just let go, but she didn't and he pulled her closer, drawing her in so hard and fast she had to push her hand against his chest to stop him. It was like fireworks exploding, sparking out from that point of contact, making her skin burn and heat race through her and she wanted to jerk her hand away, only that would make obvious the effect he was having on her, and she would rather set fire to herself than do that.

'Back off, Trip, or so help me I will call Security.'

'You mean Carlos?' He raised an eyebrow. 'I saw him on the way in, enjoying a hot dog and a frankly unfeasibly large portion of fries. No judgement. Next time I come over I'll give you a heads-up, that way he might have a chance of getting here before things get out of hand.'

A shiver spread down her spine. She knew exactly how out of hand things could get between her and Trip, and so did her body. Feeling her nipples harden, she let go of the swatch and took a step backwards, her heart racing.

'There won't be a next time,' she snapped. 'You can't seriously think I want to see you again, let alone marry you. Why would I? I don't need your money or your surname. In fact, I'm struggling to think of exactly what I would get out of your crackpot arrangement.'

She felt the ripple of that put-down spread outwards to the corners of the room, but Trip didn't react. He just stared at her, his blue gaze bright and hot and intent in a way that made her feel as if she were an animal in a trap.

'I suppose you'd get the same as you got before,' he said slowly.

There was a tense, electric moment she could feel everywhere.

She knew from the streak of colour touching his incredible cheekbones what he was talking about. Her body did too, because the air changed then. Or maybe it was the light. Whatever it was, she felt it snap taut, that quivering, electric thing between them that she'd been telling herself wasn't real.

Ignoring the heat flaring low in her pelvis, she stiffened her shoulders and met his gaze. 'That was then. This is now. Like I said earlier, I don't feel the same way as I did.'

She forced herself to hold his gaze as her lie pingponged round the room but all she was really aware of was the blue of his gaze washing over her like a wave, pulling her towards him and out into deeper, more dangerous water.

'Are you sure about that?'

Her belly clenched as he lifted his hand and smoothed her cheek, and the feel of his hand against her skin was so familiar and so irresistible that she stared up at him, mute and paralysed, incapable of convincing herself to do what was sensible and right, which would be to tell him to leave, to tell him that she was sure, could not be any surer.

But instead she said nothing. Did nothing even as he moved closer so that they were a breath apart now. His blue gaze was jewel bright on hers, striking against her skin like a match and she couldn't look away, couldn't bear to think that he would never look at her like that again.

She wanted to savour it. To let it linger on her tongue one last time, breathe in its intoxicating scent and let it roll through her like wildfire.

Maybe that was why she did nothing when he bent his head and fused his mouth to hers.

And just like that she forgot her anger and her outrage. She forgot that she was anything but a woman with needs. And as he curved his arm around her waist to pull her closer, she leaned into him, curling her fingers into the fabric of his shirt.

Oh, how she had missed this, missed him. She could feel herself melting, body softening and stirring at the same time with that same yearning need that only Trip had ever satisfied, and she wanted him so much, wanted him here, now…

As if he could read her mind or, more likely, her body, she felt his hand slide beneath the thin fabric of her blouse to find hot bare skin and her lips parted against his as his fingers stroked the swell of her breast, the nipple hardening.

It was like being on a merry-go-round, everything blurring into a shivering streak of vivid colour and hot, bright light.

She moaned softly against his mouth, and it was that sound that penetrated her brain. Suddenly she could hear Trip's voice inside her head.

'I don't remember you complaining at the time. Moaning, gasping, crying out my name, sure...but not complaining.'

And here she was again, moaning, lost in her desire and the muscle memory of those frantic, feverish months together as if he hadn't opened her up and carved out her heart while it was still beating.

She jerked her mouth away, pushing at his broad chest, and he stepped back unsteadily, releasing his grip, his blue eyes blazing with both frustration and a barely concealed triumph.

CHAPTER THREE

'WHATEVER YOU'RE ABOUT to say, don't,' Lily said hoarsely, trying to tamp down the flames crackling through her.

'Not even thank you?' His voice was mocking but there was a roughness there too, as if he was as thrown by this as she was. 'You're usually such a stickler for manners.'

She glared at him. 'Don't think this changes anything, because it doesn't.'

He started to laugh.

'I'd love to believe you, Lily, but out of the two of us you seem to be the one who doesn't know her own mind. What was it you said?' He screwed up his face as if he was trying to remember. 'Oh, yes. "I don't feel the same way as I did."'

She hated him then. But hated herself more for her lack of control, for still wanting him even at a moment like this.

Taking a breath, clinging to what was left of her pride, she met his gaze. 'Maybe I did respond to you. Because I'm human and seeing you alive made me feel things in the moment. That's all it was though, Trip, a moment. But marriage, that's about committing to someone. Sharing their life. I don't want to fake that just to help you rebrand your image. If and when I choose to get married, it's going to be to a man who understands what that entails. A man who understands me. A man who solves his own problems. Not makes them for other people. So, basically, not you.'

Heart thudding, she lifted her chin. 'You need to leave.'

He dropped back down onto the sofa once more, totally unperturbed by her words. 'And I will, but now that we're on the same page, why don't we go through our diaries? Get a date for the wedding.'

Same page? Had he not listened to a word she'd said? Clearly not.

She watched him stretch out his legs, hating him, hating the pulse of longing that still beat across her skin. He was so sure of himself. So sure of her, so sure that what had just happened was her acquiescing to his stupid plan instead of understanding that it was simply a muscle memory of that hunger they'd once shared.

Across the room, she could see the stairs that led up to her bedroom, the bedroom where Trip had stripped her naked on that very first night they'd spent together. He had stripped too with swift, expert precision, because he *would* be expert at getting naked with a woman. But she hadn't cared. She had been too busy staring at—no, drinking in—all those contoured muscles and the smooth, tanned skin and his erection, standing proud.

She had wanted him and wanted to give him everything in return in those feverish hours between dusk and dawn. But that wasn't a reason to marry him now.

Turning, she snatched up her bag. 'You're wrong,' she said with what felt like admirable calm, given that her body was still throbbing with the aftershocks of his mouth on hers. 'We're not on the same page. We're not even in the same book. And I will not be marrying you any time soon. Or ever, in fact.'

Her nerves were screaming. She'd spent the last six weeks battling her emotions, riding a roller coaster of guilt and need and grief, and now she was in the middle of processing her shock and relief at his sudden reappearance. Not that he cared about any of that. He was too busy making demands, making assumptions.

He had the gall to smile then. 'You don't have a choice. I can't take back what I said. Besides, Mason has already texted me asking when we're going to make an announcement.'

She had to press her hands against her thighs to stop herself from slapping the complacent smile from his infuriatingly handsome face.

'For the last time, there's not going to be any announcement,' she said flatly. 'Now get out of my apartment or I will call Security.'

Her breathing jerked as his eyes locked with hers. 'Why are you making this into such a big deal? It's nothing in the scheme of things. A year maybe, tops. We'd have to do a handful of public appearances together.'

'Including a wedding. Our wedding. When we'd have to lie to our family and friends. I'm not going to do that.

This is your mess, so you can sort it out. Anyway, I have plans so I'll be leaving the city. Tonight.'

He tipped back his head, back in control once again. 'What, and miss all the fun?—'

She glared at him. 'You and I have a very different idea of fun, Trip. Like I said, I leave this evening, and if you haven't spoken to these trustees and explained to them that we are not and never have been engaged by the time I touch down, then I will tell them myself.'

His eyes blazed but she was walking quickly and with purpose.

'Lily—'

He was moving now, coming after her, but she was already opening the front door. She caught a glimpse of his face, blue eyes narrowing in disbelief, and then she slammed the door, pushed the key in the lock and turned it with a rush of relief.

She couldn't be in the same room as him. Not for another second. In fact, she didn't want to be in the same city as him, the same continent even. Not when she could still feel the imprint of his mouth on hers and the burn of her own stupidity.

As she stepped into the sunlight outside, she felt a flicker of guilt at having locked him in. After all, he had only just escaped from a prison of sorts. But this was Tribeca, not Ecuador, and there was a spare key by the door. She just needed a head start and to prove that she was serious.

Even after he heard the turn of the key, it took Trip several seconds to realise what had happened.

Watching Lily lose her temper, he'd started to laugh. Because it was funny. She was so angry and outraged even though she had kissed him back.

But it had been a dumb thing to do, he knew that now. Almost as dumb as kissing her.

He scowled. It was her fault. Lily had always been so uninhibited, so passionate, so responsive to him. Not today. Today her haughty froideur had put his teeth on edge and he'd wanted to throw her off balance.

But mostly he'd just wanted to kiss her.

That was all it had taken for him to lose control. He'd forgotten why he was there in her apartment. All that had mattered was her, making her his again.

Only then she had jerked her mouth from his and he'd known from the storm in her eyes that she was furious at being proven wrong, which was no doubt why she had decided to punish him. Only by the time he'd realised that, she had already turned the key. And then he was locked in.

By the time he'd worked out what she had done he'd been too late to stop her. Even then, he'd assumed she was bluffing, that she'd wanted to have the last word, but, having called out her name a couple of times, he'd finally looked through the peephole and seen that she was gone, presumably on her way downstairs. A quick check of the street had proved that assumption correct and he'd watched, torn between disbelief and fury, as she'd looked up in the direction of the window and waved before climbing into a taxi.

Waved.

As if she didn't have a care in the world. But then she didn't. It wasn't her life, her future, that was being held in the balance.

Trip was back in his own apartment now, but by the time he'd realised Lily kept a spare key in a bowl next to the door he'd been stewing in her apartment for over an hour and a half.

He yanked open the drinks fridge, pulled out a beer, and started pacing back and forth across the huge loft space, oblivious to the dazzling view across Central Park.

He didn't like being on his own. His ADHD played a part in that. As a child he had been incapable of sitting still quietly, much to his father's irritation. Now that he was older, he had learned strategies—pacing, doodling, foot-tapping.

But there was so much going on in his head right now. He kept having flashbacks to the men in masks and his body was permanently tense with a dread he couldn't shift. And that was why this whole business with the shareholders was so unfair. Returning to New York, he had known that somebody would be holding the reins, but on his return he had assumed that he would simply take back what was rightfully his.

Only now he had the board and the shareholders on his back, and that was a real problem.

His mouth twisted. And his solution was currently planning to skip the country.

Picturing Lily's small, furious face, he winced as

his shoulders tensed and he reached round to massage his back.

He opened his eyes and stared around the light, casually elegant apartment. It was his home. Had been his home for nearly seven years and yet he hadn't thought about it once while he was out there. He hadn't thought about anything much except staying alive.

And Lily Dempsey.

His fingers tightened around the bottle. He had no idea why she'd kept popping into his head. Perhaps it was the soft rainforest air that would slide over his skin at daybreak almost like one of her caresses. Or maybe it was darkness playing tricks on his mind.

It made it even more aggravating that she was refusing to play ball. Was, in fact, threatening to talk to the trustees.

Jaw tightening, he began to pace again. That wasn't going to happen. He wouldn't allow that to happen. He couldn't. One more mess-up and there was a real risk he could lose control of the business.

'One hundred and thirty years building a business into a household name and you throw it away for a few seconds of thrill-seeking.'

His feet faltered as his father's voice sounded inside his head and some of the beer spilled onto the polished concrete floor. He frowned down at it.

Henry Winslow II had forfeited any right to sit in judgement on him, he thought, jerking the bottle to his lips. In fact, none of this would have happened if his father had been the man he'd pretended to be. It was his lies, his deceit that had set this whole mess in motion.

Without those letters he would never have accepted his friend Carter's invitation, never have ended up in a cartel hotspot.

But there was no point crying over spilt beer.

What mattered now was getting Lily to change her mind.

He felt his heart rate pick up. Outside, the sun was high above the tallest skyscrapers and the air would still be shimmering with heat.

Trip gritted his teeth. His skin was suddenly twitchy and taut. Nothing could compare to the heat of her kiss.

The effect Lily had on him was still as baffling to him today as it had been that first night. Before her, all his girlfriends had been of a type. Not through any conscious choice on his part.

But she was different.

Always slightly aloof, and serious and hard-working in a way that was unique among her more glamorous peers. Which was why it had been her name he'd plucked out of the air. She was the perfect woman to help him regain control of his business.

It was a pity, then, that she was so resistant to doing so.

He gritted his teeth.

It was all such a mess. He didn't want to get married, didn't want to have to make vows of eternal love and devotion, particularly now, after finding those letters. To do so felt wrong in so many ways.

Remembering the moment when he'd realised that the woman writing them was not his mother, he felt suddenly sick.

For a slice of a second, his mind was a flurry of thoughts, tumbling over one another, colliding, splitting apart, reforming, and he felt the same mishmash of anger and shock and pain. Because Henry wasn't perfect. He was a liar and a hypocrite and Trip was done trying to please his father, to be like his father.

Or he would be, once he had persuaded the trustees that he was the best man to run the company, and for that he needed Lily Dempsey.

But how could he persuade her?

Then again, maybe that wasn't the priority. He sat up straight. Right now, he just needed to stop her talking to the trustees. If he did that, then it would buy him some time and then he could concentrate on changing her mind.

'If and when I choose to get married, it's going to be to a man who...solves his own problems.'

Lily's voice echoed inside his head, and he got to his feet. If that was what she wanted, then that was what she was going to get. But first he needed to make a phone call.

The plane was waiting on the runway, sleek and pale grey like a gull at rest.

Lily stared at it, her throat tightening.

Her father, James, was a US senator. She was proud of him. Proud of his values and his work ethic. He was not just a charismatic speaker with catchy sound bites but a doer. Unfortunately, his job was also the reason she had been pushed into the spotlight at such a young age. It hadn't been all bad. She wasn't shy like her brother,

Lucas, and when she was very young it had been exciting to be on stage at the end of a campaign with all the balloons and the cheering.

That had all changed when certain parts of the media and the unnamed, faceless trolls had decided that she was fair game. Except it hadn't been fair, and it hadn't felt like a game. Some of the things that had been said and written about her still had the power to make her chest fill with pain, and a shame that was in itself shaming.

She had tried to keep a low profile, and sometimes that worked. Other times, she was criticised for being aloof and stuck up. But mostly they had lost interest in her because she was single, fully clothed, and the only people she let get close to her were her family and tried-and-tested friends.

Except Trip.

And look at how that was working out for her.

Fleeing felt like too strong a word, but she was definitely escaping from New York, and fortunately her father's status as Secretary of State for Veteran Affairs meant she could just hop on a plane at short notice.

She was too frazzled to feel more than a pinch of guilt. She felt safe here.

Not that Trip scared her. But the idea of people thinking they were engaged was terrifying. Worse still was the prospect of anyone uncovering the truth. That Trip had needed a name, a wife to make him look like a changed man, and had thought of her because she was reliable, sensible, unadventurous.

That should have been enough for her to throw him out of her apartment.

Instead, she'd let him kiss her.

Not just let. She had kissed him back. And that scared her too. How easily she had softened beneath his mouth. How much she had wanted to be his again in that moment.

Three crew members, two women and one man, were waiting by the stairs to greet her. She smiled politely but none of their faces were familiar. Then again, it had been nearly eighteen months since she had taken the family jet anywhere.

It would be nice to be up in the air and out of reach of everybody, she thought, tossing her bag onto one of the cream leather seats and glancing round the cabin. Was it her imagination or did the cabin seem bigger than she remembered?

Had her father changed planes?

Truthfully, she had no idea, and she certainly wasn't going to ask any of the stewards and look like some Upper East Side princess. The pilot and co-pilot chose that moment to come and introduce themselves and then it was time to fasten her seat belt. She glanced at her watch. It was a quarter to eight now, so with the time difference she should arrive in London at—

'Good evening.'

It was a man's voice and she glanced up, smiling automatically, expecting to see the male steward. The smile froze on her lips.

Trip was standing there, one hand wrapped over the

top of the seat beside her, his muscular body filling the aisle.

She stared at him, mute with shock, the memory of that feverish kiss in her apartment swelling up inside her, making her lips tingle as if it had only just happened.

He was the epitome of casual cool in a dark blue polo shirt, pale linen trousers and loafers, clothes that would have looked unremarkable on any other man. But this was Trip. It didn't matter what he wore. Nothing could diminish that shockingly sensual, dangerously masculine aura that had its own gravitational pulling power. He was the physical embodiment of a risk worth taking.

Or so she'd thought. But not any more.

'This is where you say what a surprise and a pleasure it is to see me,' he said softly.

Her throat was suddenly dry and tight, and her hands felt shaky. But, lifting her chin, she met his gaze. 'But that would mean lying and you wouldn't want to make me a liar, would you, Trip?'

'Oh, there are worse things than lying.' His voice was all smooth and silk, but there was an edge to it that made her skin tighten with warning. 'Like leaving someone locked in your apartment.' She saw his jaw tighten, just a little. 'That was a mean trick, Lily.'

'You left me no choice. You wouldn't leave,' she snapped. 'And I didn't ask you to come to my apartment, any more than I asked you to come here. Don't sit—' she added but it was too late. Trip had dropped down into the seat beside her.

She glared at him.

'What do you think you're doing? Did you not get the message?'

He shrugged and, despite her shock and rising irritation, her eyes tracked the movement of his shoulder and arm muscles.

'I get so many emails,' he said, misunderstanding her on purpose. 'But I did hear on the grapevine that we were heading in the same direction and, as you know, I'm trying to be more responsible and measured, so taking one private jet instead of two seemed like a no-brainer.'

Lily blinked. Her mind was racing. How did he know which direction she was heading? She hadn't told anyone that she was going to London except…

She felt her jaw tighten remembering how accommodating her mother had been earlier, letting her use the car and borrow the plane.

'Is that what you said to my mother?'

His blue eyes rested on her face and she saw that he looked neither remorseful nor guilty—or any of the other countless emotions he should be feeling for his behaviour, past and present. 'After you said you were leaving New York, I called her to get a few more details. Such a charming woman. Compassionate too. She's very concerned about you.' His gaze rested intently on her face. 'Apparently you haven't been yourself.'

A lump formed in her throat and for a moment she didn't trust herself to speak. How could her mother betray her like that?

Obviously she'd been devastated when she'd heard that Trip was missing, presumed dead. Equally obviously she was glad he was alive, because that was how any normal person would react.

But there were other emotions too.

Guilt, because up until the moment he'd disappeared she'd been wishing all kinds of ills would fall upon him. And fury. A dull, pounding fury that he should be so reckless, so thoughtless, so utterly solipsistic. So yes, she hadn't been herself.

'I was worried about you,' she said flatly. 'Everyone was.'

'Yeah, it's really upsetting when the stock market has a major wobble.' He stretched out his legs so that his thigh brushed against hers, not once but twice so that she knew it wasn't an accident. Gritting her teeth, she jerked her leg away.

'That's not why most people were worried. It's because they care about you.'

There was a small, prickling silence that made her skin sting. 'And were you one of those people? The ones that cared about me.'

She looked up, caught the glitter in his eyes and felt her cheeks start to burn even though she certainly shouldn't be feeling anything.

'Is that why you haven't been yourself?'

He shifted against the armrest but his gaze didn't move from her face, the slow burn of those astonishingly blue eyes of his tearing into her, seeing more than she wanted him to see.

Squaring her shoulders, she took a deep, fortifying breath. 'I'm not having this conversation with you, Trip. *No*, don't speak. I don't want to hear another word. I don't need to know what weaselly things you said to my mother so you could hitch a ride. You've had your fun and now you need to leave.'

'Can I speak now?' Trip sat back in his seat. 'Because I think you should know that isn't going to be possible. In fact, it's pretty much *im*possible given that I don't have wings or a parachute and we appear to have taken off.'

'What?'

Her head snapped round to the window and she stared through the glass in horror. Teterboro had disappeared. In its place was an endless, darkening blue sky.

She swallowed hard, then turned to face him. 'You did that on purpose. You knew the plane was taking off and you distracted me.'

He shrugged. 'I would have said something sooner, but you told me not to speak. I suppose we could ask the pilot to turn the plane around. It's a bit diva-ish, but if that's what you want to do. I'll let you do the talking—'

And say what? she thought savagely. Her head was starting to pound, and she wanted to scream. But it wouldn't alter things. There was no way she was going to ask the pilot to turn the plane around and Trip knew it.

She watched as he turned his head imperiously and one of the female stewards appeared at his elbow with almost comical speed. 'I'd like two glasses of champagne.'

'I don't want a glass of champagne,' she said through gritted teeth as the woman evaporated as swiftly as she'd appeared.

He raised one dark eyebrow. 'What's a celebration without champagne?'

She gave a small, brittle laugh. 'Strangely, having my flight hijacked by you doesn't feel like a reason to celebrate.' She was speaking calmly and precisely, as if that might change what was happening. But of course, it didn't.

'I was talking about our engagement,' he said, and his voice had a softness to it that made her shiver.

She felt her face get hot. 'We're not engaged.'

'And yet here we are. Together. Heading off into the sunset.' He glanced out of the window to where the sun was starting to slip beneath the horizon. 'It's almost as if fate is trying to tell you something. As if being "hijacked" by your fiancé is what you want. Only you don't want to admit it out loud,' he added, and, for a moment, she couldn't breathe properly.

She couldn't understand why she had thought there was more to Trip than met the eye. He was hiding in plain sight. A wealthy, powerful man who took what he wanted, when he wanted it, without any thought for the collateral damage he caused en route to satisfying his whims.

Unfastening her seat belt, she stood up. 'What I want is to be left alone.'

She snatched her bag and waited for him to move his legs, which he did with a measured slowness that made her fingers tremble. Ignoring him as best she could, she stalked down the cabin to a seat with a table beside it and spent the next hour pretending that Trip wasn't there.

But even though she was sitting with her back to

him, it was impossible not to be aware of his presence. She was like the princess in that fairy tale, and he was the pea beneath all the mattresses. As she listened to him talking to the stewards, she knew exactly how he would be sitting. Not stiffly like her, with her spine digging into the seat, but lolling easily against the leather, his chin tilted upwards, limbs arranged with a kind of louche grace that inspired both envy and longing. What was more, she could picture the cabin crew crowded round him, hanging eagerly on his every word, wide-eyed like children watching a magician perform a series of elaborate tricks.

Steadying her breathing, she reclined her seat a fraction. As well as a headache, her neck was starting to hurt with the effort of not turning round and she felt a little queasy. As a child she'd suffered terribly from motion sickness, but nowadays it was rarely a problem unless she was tired or stressed.

Her lip curled. Thanks to Trip, she was both. Luckily, she had some pills with her so maybe she would take a couple and close her eyes…

She woke up with a start.

Her mouth felt dry and her eyes felt as if they were on back to front. Light was filling the cabin, not artificial light but daylight, and outside the sky was a dazzling blue. What time was it? She glanced at her watch and jerked upright, frowning. She had assumed that she had dozed off for a couple of hours, but it was morning.

'There she is. Hey, Greta Garbo. Have a nice sleep? I tried to wake you, but you were out for the count.'

As Trip sat down opposite her, she was still too woolly-headed to do anything more than answer truthfully.

'I get motion sick sometimes, so I took a couple of pills. As soon as we land, I'll be fine.'

As soon as we land.

The words echoed inside her head and she glanced out of the window, feeling that same quivering apprehension as she had back at the apartment just before Trip had told her he wanted to marry her. Looking down at her watch again, she frowned. 'Why are we still in the air? It only takes seven hours at most to reach London.'

'True.' Trip nodded.

'So why aren't we there?'

He smiled then. 'Probably because we're not going to London.'

'What do you mean?' His answer seemed to have sucked the breath from her lungs so that her voice sounded high and thin.

Now he studied her for a long, level moment. 'We're about an hour away from a private airstrip in Siena.'

'Siena?'

'It's in Italy. Near Florence.'

'I know where Siena is,' she snapped.

In the weeks since she had last seen him, his hair had grown longer, and he pushed it back from his face. But that wasn't why her heart began to beat faster.

'I don't understand. Was there a problem? Have they had to divert the plane?' Except that didn't make any sense because Italy was further away than England.

'There's no problem.'

'Then they must have made a mistake.' She tried and failed to keep the edge of panic out of her voice. 'Why else would we be going to Italy?'

His blue gaze was bright and hot and satisfied. 'Because that's where I told the pilot to land,' he said softly.

CHAPTER FOUR

THERE WAS A slight bump that made the cabin shudder as the plane touched down and Trip was momentarily pressed back against the seat as the pilot reversed the engine thrust. Almost immediately, he heard the bark of the hydraulics balancing the steering and air pressure.

It had taken quite a few phone calls and several conversations during which he'd had to distort some of his motivations and intentions to get to this moment, but it had been worth it, Trip thought, gazing down at Lily's pale, stunned face.

'You did what?'

Her voice was frozen with shock or fury, he couldn't tell which. But then it didn't matter either way, he thought as he met her narrow-eyed gaze.

'I told the pilot to fly us to Italy.'

Glancing over at her, he saw that she was spluttering with fury, which in and of itself was immensely satisfying. He had never seen her lose control before.

His body tensed. At least not outside the bedroom.

He could still remember how stunned he'd been that first time they'd had sex.

He hadn't planned to.

They had gone for a drink at some bar with one of those huge screens showing some boxing match and nobody had even looked at them as they'd walked in. And perhaps it was that shared anonymity or maybe it was that she had looked to him to save her, but he'd forgotten that she was not his type, or that he even had a type, and they'd ended up back at her apartment, in her bed.

Eventually.

The first time they had barely got through the front door.

Before that evening, he'd thought he had her all figured out. But she had been a revelation. The sex had been a revelation. Tentative at first, then fast, urgent, clumsy almost, then hesitant again. Real, in other words, and all the more exciting for being so unscripted, so instinctive.

Watching her lose control like that had been the single most erotic experience of his life, but all he'd been to her was a pretty face.

'How dare you do that?'

He shook his head slowly. 'You deserved it—'

Her grey eyes were silver with fury. 'You're such a child,' she said after a quivering pause.

She wasn't used to losing her temper. He could tell by how she was holding herself and the tremor in her voice and he didn't like how it made him feel, knowing he was responsible. It stung that she thought he was acting out some petty vendetta.

Like so many people in his life, she had made the mistake of not taking him seriously. But now she did.

'It was your idea,' he said, making no attempt to

soften his tone. 'You said you wanted to be with a man who can solve his own problems.'

She was looking at him as if he had sprouted horns.

'And you think this is the best way to do that? By playing some stupid trick?' she said in a withering tone. As if he were extraordinarily stupid. 'Well, if you've quite finished your magic show I'm going to go and speak to the pilot and ask him to fly me back to—'

But he was done with being scolded and made to feel as if he were a fool.

'That's not gonna happen,' he said quietly. 'You see, this is *my* plane, *my* crew and they are not going to be flying you anywhere any time soon.'

Lily was still for a moment and he could see her fitting his version of the facts against hers and testing it. Now, she was shaking her head. 'No, this is my father's plane. I asked my mother if I could borrow it—'

'You did. But then I spoke to your mother and I told her that we had got engaged secretly several months ago and that was why you'd been upset. Because you'd been so worried about me, only you'd had to hide how you were feeling.' He paused and his gaze narrowed on hers in a way that made her breath go shallow. 'I explained that I thought we needed time alone together. That you were struggling to deal with everything that's happened but were too stubborn to admit it.'

'That's not true—' The fury in her voice gave it a huskiness he felt in all the wrong places, and he wanted to touch her so badly he didn't even realise that he had lifted his hand to touch her cheek.

'She was very sympathetic.'

Their eyes locked for one frozen second and then she jerked her head away from his fingers, the movement exposing the underside of her throat, the pulse beating there at a rapid pace that matched his own.

'So it's not just the trustees who think we're engaged now. Your parents do, too. In fact, your mother was all for me taking you away. She said it would be like a pre-moon.'

He was needling her as much to see her draw herself up in outrage as for any other reason. And because he liked the flush of pink it brought her cheeks and the way it made her voice grow husky. She was the only woman he'd met who was as stubborn as he was, and even though her refusal to simply accept the inevitable was frustrating as hell right now, he found himself admiring her.

Catching sight of her narrowed gaze, he felt his heartbeat start to drum inside his head. She found him equally frustrating.

And he wondered if there was something wrong with him, that he should like it so much. Like getting under her skin.

Her chin jerked up and her voice was very quiet, very furious then. 'But it's not, because that would imply we're getting married and we absolutely are *not*.'

Settling back against the leather upholstery, he gave an exaggerated shrug, mostly so that he could see the pulse in her throat accelerate. 'I don't want to argue on our pre-moon, so, if it makes you happier, let's just call it a holiday.'

He watched her clench her fists, nails digging into

the palms. 'It doesn't make me happy, and I don't want a holiday.'

'That's what people who need a holiday always say,' he murmured. 'It'll be good for you to step off the merry-go-round for a while, and the villa is a great place to relax and unwind. You can swim or sunbathe or go for a ride. Or if you want to go out there are some great restaurants in Siena, or we can take in an opera in Florence.' His eyes dropped to the pulse now beating frantically in her throat. 'Italy is a playground of the senses, so we could also just make our own entertainment—'

'I won't need entertaining because I won't be staying,' she said tightly.

Wrong, he thought, watching a spray of goosebumps spread along her bare arms. Now that she was here, there was no way he was letting Lily out of his sight until she had agreed to be his wife. Of that he was certain.

'That's what this is to you, isn't it?' Her eyes arrowed in on his face. 'Entertainment. Some kind of game. Well, it's not one I'm interested in playing. So I suggest you get *your* pilot back in here and tell him to take me back to New York.'

'That's not going to happen. And you're wrong, Lily. This isn't a game for me. It's my life. My business. My future. Which is why I released a statement announcing our engagement shortly before we left New York.' He held her gaze. 'Did you really think I'd just told your parents?'

'I don't believe you. You can't have done that—' Watching the colour drain from her face, he felt a pang of remorse. But what choice did he have? None of this was his choice. It was just the tail end of one careless decision.

'You left me no choice.'

He watched in silence as she scrolled down her phone with trembling hands. 'At least here…' he softened his voice '…you won't have to deal with the paparazzi.' She had never said as much, but he knew she had a fear and a distrust of the media, so in a way bringing her to Italy was an act of mercy.

'You have to change this. You have to call someone, tell them that you made a mistake. I can't marry you—'

The horror in her voice scraped against his masculine pride and he felt his temper flare.

'I'm not calling anyone. It's done, okay. The sooner you accept that, the sooner we can both go back to living our lives. Separately.'

He didn't know what he expected to happen. He knew what he wanted to happen, which was that she would give in, capitulate to his not unreasonable demands and agree to marry him. He felt a twinge of guilt. Okay, maybe what he had trapped her into doing was a little unreasonable, but it wasn't as if he were asking her to do something that she hadn't done a version of before.

His body hardened with predictable speed as he pictured what that version looked like, as Lily folded her arms in front of her quivering body and glared at him.

'I'm not leaving this plane.'

'One way or another you will,' he said softly.

He watched the slow rise of colour on her cheeks. 'So now you're threatening me. This is turning into quite a day for you. And for me too, seeing all these new sides to your character.'

His jaw tightened. 'It wasn't a threat. More of a point of information.' He met her gaze. 'You see, as your host I have a duty of care—'

'Did you just say duty of care?' Her grey eyes grew saucer wide. 'You're abducting me, Trip.'

Later, he would wonder what had possessed him in that moment. Maybe it was the derision in her voice or the ice in her eyes or just the fact that she didn't seem to realise how much this mattered to him, but before he realised what he was doing, he had scooped her into his arms and was walking swiftly down the aisle.

'Put me down.'

She was twisting against him, but he was already moving down the staircase towards the SUV that was waiting on the runway. Without so much as blinking, the driver stepped forward and opened the door and Trip placed her into the back seat before following her smoothly.

'Have you lost your mind?' Face burning, Lily edged to the far side of the car. 'You've no right—no right—'

She reached for the door handle, but the SUV was moving now and she looked over at the driver, not because she was expecting him to leap to her defence, but expecting some kind of reaction, shock maybe, or horror.

But the driver's eyes were fixed calmly on the road as if he was used to his boss carrying women to his car like some caveman. Maybe he was. Maybe what she called an abduction was just an ordinary day to him.

'You couldn't stay on the plane.' His voice was taut. 'And you could just give in gracefully for once. This has been a very long day.'

The headache that had started on the flight was spreading now and she pressed a thumb against the pain building at the hairline.

'You're right. Frankly, I can't wait for it to end.'

'Such urgency,' he murmured. 'So some things haven't changed.'

Looking up, she caught the glint in his eyes and felt her belly backflip as heat suffused her face and body, skin prickling with anticipation and need and fear. Fear at how easily her body could betray her, and, despite there being so much more bad to choose from, how stubbornly it continued to remember the infinitesimal amount of good.

And she could remember it all too well.

Each time they had ended up in bed it was supposed to be the last time. But then she would catch sight of him at some function or at a restaurant and it would be all she could think about.

Like that night when she'd met up with some girlfriends at Piatto for dinner.

Trip had been there with his father and, though she hadn't gone over to talk to him, just knowing he was there had made the restaurant floor feel as if it were on an angle and she'd had to press her chair down into the floor to stop it sliding towards him.

He'd left the restaurant first, but he had been outside, waiting for her just as she had waited for him that first time. She felt her pulse fluttering, remembering the throb of the blood in her veins as they'd walked on opposite sides of the street, not looking at each other but so intensely aware of every step the other took that it had been as if they were joined by an invisible thread.

As they'd turned the corner, he had abruptly crossed the road and she had pulled him against her, the dark impatience in his eyes and the feel of his mouth on hers unleashing that hunger that shivered inside her, a hunger that she should have resisted because she knew the risks, particularly with a man like Trip.

But looking into his eyes, she had been sure he wasn't pretending. That he felt what she did.

Until he didn't, and then he'd ended it, and now he only wanted her because she was safe and dull. And because her parents believed in love, the head-over-heels kind that made you act like a fool and risk everything, and because they wanted her to be happy, they had accepted his lies.

They didn't know he was faking it.

But she did.

Shifting her body towards the car door, she stared helplessly into the fading light. So why did she still want to lean closer to him? To touch, explore, caress, kiss…

She felt flushed with the heat of it, and her voice was scratchy when she replied. 'Everything's changed. Except you. You never change. Which is why you're in the mess you're in.'

The blue gleam of his gaze made her breath catch.

'You know what your problem is? It's all this thinking in absolutes. Everything. Always, never—it's exhausting. No wonder your parents think you need a break.'

Her shoulders were aching, muscles tensing from the effort of holding in the scream of frustration that was building inside her. Balling her hands, she inched closer to the door. 'If I'm exhausted it's because of you, because of this.'

She was lucky. She had a family she loved and who loved her. A job she adored. A small but close group of friends. A beautiful, spacious apartment and enough money to never have to think about money.

So why had she spent so much of her life living in the shadows?

Not all her life. Trip had been sunlight on her face, and she had basked in it greedily, gratefully, even though she knew that sunlight couldn't be trusted. That looking into it left you blinded and dazed so that you couldn't see what was right in front of you.

Like with Cameron.

He wasn't as traffic-stoppingly beautiful as Trip, but he was cool and edgy and popular and she had been flattered by his attention, intoxicated with the entirely new sensation of being one of the in crowd, so that it had only been later that she'd realised he couldn't be trusted.

By then the damage had been done. She had put her brother in harm's way, encouraging him to drive them all back to the city even though Cameron had told her weeks earlier that he didn't own a car. But it hadn't seemed important until she'd heard the police sirens.

She'd tried to explain, but the fact was the car had been stolen. By the time her father had arrived at the police station, Lucas couldn't stop shaking and he was crying too hard to answer questions. And the worst part had been that both her parents were so understanding.

No, actually the worst part had been Lucas going to the clinic in Geneva.

Her heart was beating in her throat.

It had taken a long time to forget the terror and misery of that night. But sometimes even now if they heard a police siren she would see Lucas' hands shake and his face stiffen with panic and she would want to cry. He had always been highly strung and shy and struggled with debilitating anxiety, but now he was reclusive.

As for her…

Over the years, all the sneering remarks about her appearance had left her cautious around people in general, and men in particular, but she had thought Cameron was different. That he had seen her inner beauty whereas, in fact, with one cool, assessing glance he had spotted the lonely girl who lived inside her who wanted someone to notice her. Talk to her. Think she was special.

The interior of the car shuddered in and out of focus as if she were sitting inside a snow globe and someone were shaking it. Her face felt hot with shame.

Which was why sleeping with Trip had been such a crazy thing to do. At least the risks she'd taken had not impacted anyone else. And nobody had been there to see how easy he'd found it to abandon her. As she remembered his haste to be gone, her breath felt ragged.

She felt his gaze on her face.

'And I don't have any problems,' she lied. 'Except you,' she added. 'You're my problem.'

'That's progress,' he said softly. 'Yesterday I wasn't your anything.'

He shifted against the leather upholstery and every single nerve ending in her body twitched in unison and it was so intense that she had to stop herself from pulling off her seat belt, throwing open the car door and leaping onto the road as they did in the movies.

She turned her face towards the window, seeing nothing, body taut with frustration, furious with herself for telling him what she was going to do and thereby giving him an opportunity to set this 'plan' in motion.

When he'd broken up with her, she had thought he was self-centred, arrogant and entitled, but this was a whole new level of impossible to process behaviour. He had lied to her parents, lied to her, tricked her into thinking she was on her way to London when all the time he was bringing her here.

Her gaze fixed on the distant hills with their patchwork fields of green and gold.

'Exactly where are you taking me?' she demanded, turning towards him.

'Villa Morandi. My father's villa. Mine now, I guess.' He seemed almost surprised, as if that thought had only just occurred to him, and there was an edge to his voice that hadn't been there before.

She had met Henry on a handful of occasions. Outwardly, Trip resembled his father in the broadest strokes. The height, the fine, straight nose and the blue eyes. But their personalities could not be more different. Henry had been all about planning and projections. He had been autocratic, disciplined and focused on the prize.

Whereas Trip brought the energy and excitement into any room. He took chances—or risks, depending on your perspective.

But Trip was still his son, and for many boys, their father was a guide into manhood. Was that why he was acting like this? Because he had lost his polestar? She wanted to ask, to reach out and smooth that rigidity from his shoulders, but that would mean having to touch him and it would be beyond stupid of her to do that.

'And what would he think about you doing this?' She made her voice neutral, in the way she'd learned from watching her own father deal with political opponents and critics. 'I spent time with your father. He didn't act on impulses. He thought things through, and he left you in charge of his business so I'm guessing he wanted you to step up. To grow up and be a worthy successor. I'm certain he didn't expect you to marry someone against their will.'

He was watching her blandly, but now the light in his gaze sharpened in a way that made her breath go shallow and she knew she had landed a blow.

'Fine, so break up with me. Here, you can use my phone.' He tossed it across the seat. 'Make it official. Call your father. I should warn you, though, there's a fair amount of blood in the water, so the sharks are already circling. You tip in some chum, and it'll turn into a feeding frenzy real fast. Because it isn't just my image that's going to be affected by our splitting up.'

She stared at him, her heart beating out a drumroll of panic against her ribcage.

He was right. Headlines involving words like 'sena-

tor's daughter' and 'break-up' would make people sit up
and take notice. Add in a photo of Trip looking louche
and sexy stepping off a plane after his miraculous return
from the dead and the story could run for days, weeks,
months in the summer's slow news cycle.

It would be the ultimate clickbait.

Despite her attempts to stop it, a shiver ran down her
spine as she imagined the trolling that would start the
minute the story broke.

What fun they would have. Imagine, they would say,
that Lily Dempsey thought she could enchant a man like
Trip Winslow. Because it wouldn't matter what statement they put out, everyone would assume she'd been
dumped. All the old pictures would be rolled out. The
ones that made her want to curl into a ball beneath her
duvet. No place had been beyond the intrusive reach of
their lenses. No topic was taboo. Not her hair or dress
sense. Not even her weight or the straightness of her
teeth.

But she could cope with that, had been coping with
it since she was nine years old and her father's career
had apparently made her public property.

'But hey, you know that though, don't you?' Trip said
then. 'You and your family know all about managing
reputation and image. Why else would the world think
your brother was learning musical composition at the
Conservatoire in Paris three years ago, when in fact he
was in Switzerland?'

Lily's eyes flew to his and everything inside her
lurched as if the car had hit a pothole in the road. She
knew she had gone white. Could feel the blood drain-

ing away. Nobody outside the family knew about Lucas' time in the clinic. Their father had driven him there himself.

'You don't know anything—'

He made an impatient sound. 'No, I don't. And neither do those photographers and reporters who are currently sleeping in their cars outside my apartment. But knowing things that other people don't know is how they make their living. Once they find a loose thread, they keep pulling on it until it unravels. Or snaps.'

There was a different note to his voice now. A kind of quiet firmness. Like a door closing that couldn't be opened from the inside.

Lily felt sick. Outside the sunlight was too bright to look into directly, but there were shadows beneath the trees and she could feel the darkness outside seeping towards her.

She had been thinking about herself.

Only it wouldn't just be her, it would be her family, too, who would be caught in the net. That was fine for her parents. Her father had chosen his career and her mother had chosen her father knowing who he was and where his ambitions lay, but Lucas…

Picturing her brother's face, she felt her ribs tighten.

He was the polar opposite of Trip. Shy, self-effacing, sensitive, not at all comfortable in his beautiful skin.

Not that Trip knew or cared about that. And in some ways, it was irrelevant now that their engagement was official. Trip had been the big news story for the last twenty-four hours, and the revelation that he and Lily were secretly engaged would be catnip to the press packs.

Picturing them jostling for position on the stoop outside her apartment, she shuddered. She hated being in
the limelight, but Trip had made that an inevitability. So,
she had a choice, if you could call it that. Stay engaged
and hope the media focused on the upcoming wedding
and the bridal excesses of the Upper East Side. Or break
up with Trip and wait for the sky to fall on her head.
Because it would. And not just her head. The impact of
ending things with someone so high profile would be
impossible to contain.

Being caught in the wake of the media madness that
would follow her 'dis-engagement' would be horren-
dous for Lucas, but if someone pulled on one of his
loose threads...

Thanks to her last doomed decision to trust someone, he was still fragile, more so even than was usual.

She couldn't risk him unravelling again. Or worse.

There was a beat of silence, then another.

Clenching her hands so tightly that her nails dug into
her palms, she lifted her chin. 'How long would I have
to do it for? Be married to you, I mean.'

There was a short, pulsing silence.

'I hadn't really got that far. A year, I suppose. Maybe
a little longer.' She had assumed Trip would be elated.
This was, after all, his moment of triumph, but as his
gaze moved from her face to her tightly closed fist, she
could see a muscle working in his jaw. 'Does it really
matter?'

No, not at all, she thought, turning towards the darkness, letting it swallow her up and blot out the panic
in her chest and throat. If she could survive a day, she

would survive any number and she *would* survive. She had to.

'What matters is that we broke the news of our engagement to suit our agenda. You see, there's a way to do these things. Announcing it when all this other stuff about my "return" is dominating the news means that people are going to concentrate on the positives. That's good for you too, Lily.'

Was it? She stared at him dully, not even caring that he so casually used 'we' and 'our' as if this were some carefully negotiated agreement instead of a unilateral ambush.

Because now she knew what mattered. Not her feelings. Not the trajectory of her life. But was that so surprising? She already knew there was a perceived association in most people's minds between being attractive and being important. Although they had started before she was a teenager, the years of being mocked and being made to feel inferior because her nose had a bump on it and her hair wasn't smooth and glossy were not some distant memory.

It hurt to have confirmation that Trip felt that way about her. To know that he had found it so easy to break up with her and just as easy to now manipulate her into this charade of a marriage.

She didn't know how long the rest of the journey took. It felt endless. Felt as if time had stopped and she was simply reliving the same moment over and over again. Finally, the car took a little twist to the left onto a road that led onto a drive edged with cypress trees.

And then she saw it.

Framed by the Tuscan countryside, the Villa Morandi looked like an enchanted palace from a fairy tale. Her heartbeat accelerated as the driver slowed the car, then turned off the engine and walked around to open her door. Stepping out onto the driveway, she gazed up mutely at the villa, her eyes moving appreciatively over the sun-faded walls and dark green shutters.

'What do you think?'

Trip's voice snapped her thoughts in two and she turned to face him. 'It's lovely,' she said truthfully. She had wanted to hate it, but it felt wrong to lie.

Wrong to lie? Her heart began to race again. What was wrong with her? Trip had not just lied to her, he had misled the trustees and manipulated her parents and was forcing her into a marriage of his convenience for which he had shown zero contrition. She needed to toughen up, and fast, or she was never going to survive this.

Lifting her chin, she gave the villa another cursory glance, then shrugged. 'But if you've seen one Italian villa, you've seen them all. I mean, they all look the same. Their owners do, too. Let's hope I don't get you mixed up with some other self-absorbed, manipulative billionaire.'

'That would complicate things.' His blue eyes glinted in the sunlight and she felt his gaze sweep over her. 'But given that we spent most of our time together naked, perhaps we should just take off all our clothes. That way there would be no confusion.'

There was no answer to that, and she turned away from the house.

Now that the shock of being there had faded a little,

her senses felt as though they were being bombarded. A hot, dry breeze was caressing her skin and she could smell the earth and the grass and the cypress trees and, beyond the trees, she could hear…

Nothing.

Her body tingled. She was surrounded by silence, and she had a feeling she'd never had before. Of being far from civilisation, because she didn't need a map to know there was nothing for miles in every direction.

She shivered. There was nothing here except forced intimacy with the man standing beside her, and that thought made the darkness and the heat and the silence press in on her so that it was suddenly difficult to breathe.

A slight middle-aged woman with long, greying hair in a ponytail stepped forward to greet them with a smile on her face. 'Buongiorno, Signor Winslow, Signorina Dempsey,' she said. 'I hope you had a pleasant flight.'

'There was a little turbulence, wasn't there, darling?' Trip turned to her and gave her a smile that didn't reach his eyes. 'But nothing we couldn't handle.

'Lily, this is Valentina. She's the housekeeper and estate manager. Anything you need or want, start with her. Except tonight.' He turned towards the older woman. 'Thanks, Valentina. I can take things from here.'

As they walked through the hall, Trip turned towards her. 'I'll let you get settled in and then we can have something to eat.'

Eat? How could he think about eating?

Lily stared at him blankly, suddenly light-headed. In the car, when she had agreed to marry him, it hadn't felt real. But now it did. It was actually happening, only this was just the beginning.

'I'm not hungry,' she said coolly. 'I want to lie down. And don't for one minute think that you'll be lying beside me.'

He raised an eyebrow but all he said was, 'I'll show you to your room.'

Heart pounding with misery and exhaustion, she followed him upstairs, her pulse accelerating wildly as he led her into a charming bedroom with a beautiful carved four-poster bed.

'This is where you're sleeping.'

She froze as he turned to face her. There was enough space between them to park a car and yet the taut, masculine power of his body was too close for comfort.

'There's a bathroom through there, and this is the dressing room.' As he stepped forward a light clicked on softly overhead and her eyes narrowed, not on Trip, but on a jacket hanging from the rail. She had one just like it—

Her breath caught in her throat as she stared at the other clothes that had been neatly folded and hung.

'Where did you get these?'

'Your mother had them sent over to my apartment before we left.'

Another betrayal. Wincing inwardly, and needing distance from his disturbingly piercing gaze, she backed out of the dressing room into the bedroom and walked towards the floor-to-ceiling picture window.

The drapes were open and she stared through the glass. Her eyes felt hot. It was strange to think that this was the same sun that she had watched set in New York yesterday afternoon. It seemed so much brighter, like a sun in a dream. Her fingers bit into the skin of her wrist. If only she could pinch herself awake from the nightmare that was engulfing her.

'You know it's not just me, Lily.'

Trip was standing behind her. She could see his reflection in the window, but she would have known he was there even if she'd been blindfolded. That thread again.

Their eyes met in the glass and she saw his pupils flare, felt it like a flicker of heat low in her belly, impossible to ignore, imperative to resist.

'Everyone wants this for us. You wanted it too. Wanted me.'

She felt something rough-edged scrape inside her and she wanted to back away, hide in the dressing room, but there would be no point. She couldn't hide from the truth, from that heat pulsing across her skin and the tightness inside her. And it was true. She had wanted him.

More than wanted him.

In those hours when they had been alone in her apartment he had been essential to her. Like air and water and sunlight. It had been beautiful too and even though she'd known it would end, could never be anything more than it was, it had been hers, and it had worked, the raw sensuality, that hunger, being wanted like that. Only now he was making the memory of it ugly.

'The idea of it, yes,' she said coolly, without bothering to turn around. 'But most women have any number of romantic fantasies in their head and the trouble with fantasies is that they're always a bit of a let-down.'

For a moment he didn't reply, and then he reached into his pocket and pulled out a small, square box.

Her heart gave a little jerk as he opened it and she stared down at the huge marquise diamond surrounded by smaller sapphires. 'But this isn't a fantasy. It's a means to an end. We need to be engaged. Both of us. Which is why, from now on, you need to wear this.'

He held out the ring and as if hypnotised, she took it and slid it onto her fourth finger.

Trip was staring at her hand. 'Does it fit okay?'

She nodded and she wondered briefly how he knew what size to choose. 'It feels strange,' she said stiffly.

His gaze lifted to her face, the blue of his irises one shade darker than the stones in her ring.

'You'll get used to it.' He hesitated as if he had some-thing else to say, but then he turned and she watched him walk away. He stopped at the door to remove the key and then he was shutting the door and she waited for the click of the lock, but she heard nothing.

Because he didn't need to lock her in. She wasn't going anywhere and he knew it, and it was all too easy to hate Trip then. Only hating him didn't change any-thing. He might have lied to her, tricked her, abducted her and blackmailed her. But she was still going to have to marry him.

CHAPTER FIVE

'WOULD YOU LIKE some more tea, *signorina*?'

Glancing up at Valentina, Lily shook her head. 'No, thank you. I only ever have one cup.'

She shifted position in her chair and returned her gaze to where it had been fixed for the last twenty minutes to a point about an inch to the left of Trip's maddeningly handsome face.

They were having breakfast outside beneath swathes of fragrant wisteria.

Beyond the formal gardens with their box hedging and parterres and half-hidden statuary was a rippling landscape of greens in every shade uninterrupted by anything man-made. Just paddocks of grazing horses, rows of olive trees and sloping fields of grape-covered vines and then finally the dark bosky hills that rolled up to meet the cloudless blue sky.

It was her first meal at the villa and the food was excellent, on a par with anything her parents' housekeeper, Marisa, produced back in New York. She was still a little too tense to fully enjoy her breakfast of delicately scrambled eggs with curling ribbons of crispy pancetta, but that wasn't Valentina's fault. She seemed like a nice person and she wasn't responsible for the actions of her capricious owner.

'The eggs were wonderful, by the way,' she said, glancing up at the housekeeper and smiling. 'And the bread. In fact, it was all delicious.'

Yesterday, probably because of the stress and the left-over effects of anti-nausea pills, she had fallen asleep and unintentionally missed lunch. Waking in the late afternoon, she had showered and changed clothes and, drawn to the miraculous view from her window, she had decided to leave the sanctuary of her room.

Only then had she caught sight of Trip wandering in the garden, looking irritatingly relaxed and handsome, talking on the phone, and she had felt so furious that she had picked up her own phone to call her mother and tell her the truth.

But, swiping right, she had been confronted by the screensaver of her family and, gazing down into her brother's sweet face, had felt her anger ooze away.

At some point, Trip had knocked on the door and called out her name softly and she had sat, muscles quivering, poised to dart into the bathroom, which at least had a key. He hadn't come in and she had spent the next few hours alternately hating him and trying to come up with some way to extricate herself without causing collateral damage to everyone she loved.

She failed.

Later, she had watched Valentina set a beautiful candlelit table with a mounting sense of dread as the reality of what she'd agreed to had set in. Maybe Trip had read her mind because it had been the housekeeper who'd knocked on her door that time. She'd opened it and explained that she had a migraine and would not be joining Mr Winslow for supper.

It had felt like a minor victory, albeit in a war she had already conceded. But this morning, gazing out at the mist-covered hills, she had decided that she was done with hiding. She had spent so much of her life keeping her head down, trying not to be seen, not even for the things that she was good at, like her job.

And if anyone should be hiding away it was Trip. It was that thought that had propelled her downstairs and through the elegant sitting room with its marble-topped side tables and exquisite linen-covered sofas.

It was the right thing to do, she told herself. The warm, lemon-scented air was calming and, despite its elegance, the blush-pink house was a comforting backdrop. Hidden slightly by a hedge of paintbrush-tipped cypresses, a shimmering blue swimming pool glittered temptingly like a sapphire in the sunshine.

But the pool and the house were still overshadowed by the breathtaking beauty of its owner, she thought, watching through lowered lashes as Trip shifted back in his chair to squint up at the Tuscan sun that was partly to blame for that annoying but undeniable truth.

Given his behaviour, it should be hiding behind a cloud. Instead, the sun seemed determined to show Trip in his best light, illuminating the extraordinary sculpted angles and curves of his face like a master cinematographer.

Turning her face minutely away from the gravitational pull of his flawless features, she stared deter-

minedly to where the horses, coats gleaming, were
tossing their heads fretfully to dispel any curious flies.
It looked exactly like—

'It looks like a painting, doesn't it?'

Trip's voice cut across her thoughts and, pulse stumbling, she turned towards him, jolted that he could read
her mind. Not that it was the first time. Only then she
had wanted him to. Now it didn't seem fair that he re-
tained that power.

For Valentina's benefit, she gave an infinitesimal nod
of her head. 'I suppose it does.' She had no intention of
letting him know that he could see inside her head. Or
of making this easy for him in any way.

He had thought she would, of course. Coming downstairs this morning, he had acted just as if they were
here on holiday. As if this trip were something consensual, something they had discussed with excitement
together, when in reality she had been pushed into a corner, trapped into a year-long charade against her will.

Not that Trip cared, she thought, glancing across the
table to where he was lounging in the seat opposite her,
handsome in pale chinos and a fine pale blue shirt. Now
that he had got his own way he seemed to have completely forgotten what he had done to reach this point.

So maybe it was time to remind him.

As Valentina disappeared back into the house, Lily
put down her cup.

'Just a point of information. I know you're not a details kind of guy, but if this is going to work, then you
need to understand that there have to be some ground
rules for our "arrangement". My rules.'

'You have rules for this?' That mouth of his curved
into something that wasn't quite a smile, something that
banged through her like falling scaffolding. 'And there
was me thinking I was your first.'

Her temper flared.

'You think this is a joke? You've put me in an impossible position. That's why I've agreed to do this, Trip,
and I will make the best of it. But the best version of
this for me will be to spend as little time as possible
with you.'

He studied her for a moment. 'You are aware that
we're going to be married?'

There was that same slight curve pulling at his mouth
as if her words didn't matter to him. But as he stretched
out his legs there were different truths layered beneath
his casual manner. She could see them in the slight narrowing of his eyes and the sudden elevation of tension
in that mouth-watering body of his.

'I understand that we will have to spend time together
in public, and when that happens, I will behave the way
that couples do in a real relationship. You know, the kind
where one party hasn't been coerced into the relationship by the other.'

He eyed her across the table. 'But our way is so much
more stimulating, don't you think?'

She ignored him. 'I will make conversation and smile
but, just so we're clear, that doesn't mean that I want to.'
And she wasn't going to let him forget it. 'I don't want
anything from you, except my freedom. Unfortunately,
you've made me a co-conspirator to your lies, but that
doesn't mean I have to lie when we're alone. So I won't

be making small talk with you when we're on our own. It's bad enough that I'm going to have to play-act in public. I won't do it in private.'

Private. The word jangled inside her head, made her think of low lighting and locked doors, and her stomach cartwheeled, nipples tightening as every single cell in her body quivered into a state of such heightened awareness that just meeting his gaze made her feel dizzy.

'Nor are there going to be any "benefits" between us,' she said stiffly, trying to sound like the opposite of the woman who had melted against him less than forty-eight hours ago.

'Benefits?'

The skin on her face felt suddenly too tight. 'You know, intimacies,' she said quickly, ignoring the pulse of heat that beat up over her throat and face as her brain unhelpfully suggested the range of acts that word might include.

Steadying her breathing, she pushed back her seat. 'And now that we both know where we stand, I'm going to—'

'What about kissing?' He frowned. 'What's the rule about that?'

'What?' Lily tensed all the way through.

'Kissing?' he repeated, his eyes finding hers. 'Does that count as intimate?'

'Of course it does,' she said quickly.

'Then I'm confused,' he said, mildly enough but there was a gleam in those blue eyes of his that she felt everywhere. 'Because the other day when we kissed at your apartment, we were one hundred per cent on our own.'

That shimmering thread between them pulled taut as she realised too late that she had stepped into a trap of her own making. There was no answer to that. Or none that she was willing to share with Trip, here in the beautiful Italian sunshine.

At the time she had been lost in the moment and the press of his mouth on hers and the scent of his skin.

It was only afterwards that she had attempted to rationalise her behaviour as something that had needed to be done. So not rational, but understandable. Because she had hated how it had ended before, with her telling him that she didn't care what he did or where he went. Or even if he came back.

Kissing had felt right, and the rightness of it and the fierceness of it had taken her breath away, and all of it, all her anger and hostility, had melted away and there had just been heat and need and truth.

Only now there was nothing but lies.

'There will be no kissing at all,' she hissed, getting to her feet. 'If we have to look like a couple, we can hold hands.'

'And why would we have to do that?' His gaze was so blue, so deep, she felt as though she were drowning. 'Just for information purposes, of course,' he called after her as she stalked back into the house.

She stayed upstairs until lunchtime. When Valentina knocked on the door to tell her the meal was ready she was tempted to pretend she had another migraine, but she couldn't do that every single time Trip annoyed her. Clutching a novel in front of her like a shield, she followed the housekeeper downstairs.

Lunch was light but just as delicious as breakfast. As one of the maids arrived to clear the table, she was fully intending to retreat to her room to read. Trip had other ideas.

'We'll take coffee by the pool. It's cooler down there. More private,' he added, reaching out to take her hand, no doubt in retaliation for her words at breakfast. She had no option but to let him, but as soon as Valentina had deposited their coffee onto one of the tables by the sunloungers she snatched her hand away again.

Of course, she didn't need to worry. Trip needed constant stimulation and within five minutes he had disappeared back into the villa.

Tipping her head back, she gazed up at the cloudless blue sky and then quickly looked back down again. It was too much like looking into Trip's eyes. Reaching down, she picked up her book and opened it. A light breeze was moving in from the mountains and, liking the feel of it against her skin, she half closed her eyes.

That was better…

'So what would be the next step?'

Her eyes snapped open and she stared across the rectangle of glittering blue water. Trip was back, a satellite phone pressed against his smooth dark head, sunlight dancing across his face as if it were delighted to see him.

Oh, and he had changed into black swim shorts. *Great.*

She stared at him, dry-mouthed, conscious suddenly that she was not quite controlling her reaction, but thankfully he was walking away from her, pacing back and forth along the length of the pool, moving with that familiar mesmerising athletic grace. Judging by the tension in his shoulders, it was a business call, although she didn't really care one way or another. Nothing about Trip was of any interest to her.

Liar, she thought, a beat of heat looping down to her stomach and back up to her throat as she tried not to stare at his semi-naked body.

She hadn't forgotten how gorgeous he was, but it was still a shock to be within spitting distance of all that bare, golden skin and curving muscle.

Not that she wanted to spit. She wanted to press her lips against his chest and follow the trail of fine dark hairs with her tongue to where they disappeared beneath the waistband of his trunks. Then go lower still to where the hairs thickened, and keep licking until they were both panting and mindless with hunger.

Her throat was so dry now it hurt to swallow and she could feel the back of the chair pressing against her spine. Just for a moment, she allowed her gaze to rest on the ripple of muscle but then it was too much.

Gripping the book tighter, she ducked her head and stared blindly at the words, seeing nothing, reading nothing, her body twitching restlessly against the lounger.

Trip was still pacing, but now he stopped so that he was in profile to her, the outline of his body silhouetted crisply against the blue of the sky, taut, lean, undeniably male. It was no surprise to her and yet she felt the shock of it curl through her body as hot colour flooded her cheeks when he glanced over and found her watching him.

'I have to go,' he said softly.

Jerking her gaze away, she stared back down at the lines of type, her heart bumping against her ribs as he came closer.

There was a slight creak as he sat down. She could see his body out of the corner of her eye, but it was his scent that was playing havoc with her nerve endings.

'What are you doing?' Her fingers fumbled against the book and she had to flatten herself against the cushions as he suddenly got to his feet and leaned over her.

'Calm down.' His eyes narrowed on her face. 'I'm not going to jump you.'

'You did before.' She swallowed, hard, remembering the heat, the fire, the devastating rush of need, her own unthinking impatience to walk through the flames with him. 'And then you tricked me into flying here with you and you've done nothing but threaten and bully and manipulate me ever since, so you'll forgive me if I'm a little hazy about your intentions.'

He held up his hands as if he were the one being threatened.

'I was just moving the parasol.' He gestured up towards the bleached-out sun high above them. 'So that you don't get burned.' His blue eyes rested on the blouse and pants she was wearing. 'Although you might actually die of heatstroke before that happens. Are you not hot?'

Lily smiled thinly.

Thanks to her mother, she was, because, aside from the jacket she had recognised, Laura had packed the kind of clothes that would be suitable for a romantic holiday à deux. Which was, of course, what her mother thought this was.

She gritted her teeth. Only she didn't want to wear some conspicuously new and humiliating unworn skimpy bikini or semi-transparent dress in front of Trip any more than she wanted to make small talk with him. Which was why she was dressed in the same clothes that she had worn on the plane. Because, despite the heat of the day, she needed her armour.

'I'm fine, thank you,' she said stiffly.

Trip stared down at her for a moment, his blue gaze momentarily hotter than the sun, and then he shrugged. 'Suit yourself.'

She held his gaze. 'Nothing about this situation suits me, Trip, as you very well know.'

She half expected him to respond but he was already turning towards the pool, and she watched with a mix of fury and envy as he dived into the water. It was the kind of dive that barely made a ripple on the glassy surface, which had to be a first for him, she thought, her heart still beating out of time from that last interaction.

Partly it was the fact that he was one of the richest men in the world, partly it was his extraordinary looks, but there was more to Trip than just the obvious. He had an energy, a presence that changed the atmosphere around him, making it shimmer and ripple like the air above roads in a heatwave. She had seen first-hand how he could cause a kind of seismic ripple to the structure of any building he was in. Even when his muscular outline was distorted by the water, there was something that kept pulling your gaze towards him. Anticipation, maybe, for the moment when he would emerge, god-like, from the water.

As if on cue, he did just that, pulling himself up onto the tiled edge of the pool with effortless grace. Her pulse ticced in her throat as he smoothed back his wet hair, sending water trickling down the hard planes and angles of his back and shoulders.

It was impossible to look away, excruciating to keep looking.

So move, she told herself, but Trip was already walking towards her and then he was sitting beside her, stretching out one long muscular leg and tilting his head up to the sun.

'Ah, here's Valentina,' he said softly, and before she had a chance to react he had taken her hand and lifted it to his mouth.

The housekeeper had brought out a jug of freshly squeezed peach juice and, pressing her lips together in a tight smile, Lily sat fuming while Trip dragged out the conversation on purpose by asking Valentina which peaches she had used. And the whole time, he caressed the back of Lily's hand with his thumb in a way that made her feel restless and light-headed.

Finally, Valentina left and Lily jerked her hand free of his grip and got shakily to her feet.

He glanced up at her, frowning. 'What are you doing?'

'I'm going indoors.'

'For real?' His face was expressionless, but she could hear the frustration in his voice. 'Why? Because I held your hand? I'm following your rules. Maybe you should too, Lily, because you need this to work as much as I do. If it doesn't, I think life is going to be real hard for you and everyone you care about, so stop fighting me and stop fighting yourself, because this is happening.'

He was right on both counts, she thought as she headed back into the house for the second time that day. But knowing that didn't make it any easier to live with.

Staring after her, Trip felt his hands curl into fists. Yesterday had been a challenging but ultimately satisfying day. Obviously Lily had been furious with him and it had taken longer than he'd thought for her to stop fighting him. But then he'd mentioned Lucas and she had acquiesced with a speed that had confused him.

And unsettled him.

Picking up the jug of peach juice, he poured himself a glass and drank it swiftly. Normally, he found the familiar sweetness calming but now it sat in his stomach like a lump of ice.

He knew Lily's younger brother. Not well, but enough to know that he was shy and sensitive and probably not equipped to handle the modern media machine. Nor did he know for sure what Lucas had been doing in Zurich, and to be truthful he probably would have never given it a second thought. But then he'd realised that the Dempseys had lied about Lucas' whereabouts.

There had been no need to join the dots for him to work out why. Among his set there was only one reason people lied about being in Zurich. It was because they were in rehab.

He hadn't ever planned on using it as leverage, but then Lily wouldn't give in and he'd been getting impatient. And working and living with Henry Winslow II had taught him that if you found a crack, you pushed on it to see what, if anything, broke.

And Lily had capitulated.

But as victories went, it had been less than satisfying. She had looked small and fragile, just like that time at the auction, and, watching her face grow pale, he hadn't liked how it made him feel. It wasn't who he was, whatever she might think. He was impulsive, occasionally thoughtless, sometimes arrogant, but he didn't lie or cheat or bully or blackmail or do any of the other things she had accused him of doing.

And he didn't want to hurt Lily. In part that was one of the reasons he'd decided to bring her to Italy.

Because something had happened to him in Ecuador. It might be a cliché but staring down the barrel of a gun had rewired him in some way. All those weeks of feeling vulnerable and alone had made him understand that he could rely only on himself. That he needed to be ruthless. Single-minded. Selfish even.

And then there were the letters. Lily had been the first person he'd seen after reading them and shock had made him colder, and crueller, than he should have been. More like the man he couldn't not love, but resented and hated. Knowing that had angered him, and he'd felt guilty too for taking it out on Lily, but in the moment it had been easier to blame her for making him feel so out of control.

He'd done the same thing earlier today, his guilt at dragging her into all of this colliding with his frustration at her continuing and pointless refusal to accept the new status quo, and so he'd lashed out at her with the kind of ultimatum Henry had specialised in. And he hated being like his father.

Tilting back his head, he stared into the sun until everything turned white and he was forced to blink. If only he could blank out those pages, unsee those lines of cursive script, but he couldn't.

It was what he'd hoped would happen in Ecuador. But the blindfold and then the silence and claustrophobic gloom of the jungle had simply made everything inside his head sharper and louder. He'd thought he was going to lose his mind. Only one thing had kept him going: Lily.

He had dreamed about her constantly, often with such clarity that when he'd woken he'd half expected to find her by his side. And when, finally, he'd escaped his captors it had been her eyes that had been like silver stars guiding him onwards whenever he couldn't see the night sky through the rainforest canopy.

His shoulders tensed.

Obviously, he hadn't been himself in those days and weeks in the jungle, but in some ways it made sense for him to have imagined Lily. After all, he had ended up in her apartment every night for months, right up until he'd left for Ecuador.

No doubt that was also why hers had been the first name to pop into his head when he'd been squaring up to Mason and the other trustees.

Not that he was planning on explaining any of this to Lily. He didn't need to.

She hadn't come quietly or easily, but she was here

now, with her rules and that tilt of her chin. And her un-canny ability to find the cracks in his armour.

Remembering how she had thrown his father's name at him like some verbal gauntlet, he gritted his teeth.

'And what would he think about you doing this?' Lily had asked. *'He wanted you to step up. To grow up.'*

The answer to that question made him get to his feet abruptly, because it wasn't Lily's voice inside his head, but Henry's, and his chest clenched, tightening hard, tightening around an emptiness that was as familiar as it was painful. He swayed forward. His brain felt as if it were short-circuiting and his hands moved automati-cally to his face, but it would take more than tapping to quiet his mind. He turned and began to walk swiftly away from the house.

Rereading the same paragraph for the umpteenth time, Lily looked up from her book and sighed. She was sit-ting on the window seat in her room and it was in many ways the perfect spot to read. Light but not bright, comfy enough to relax but not to doze off. But she couldn't concentrate. All she could think about was what Trip had said to her earlier.

He was right. She did need this to work. No doubt, news of their engagement would leak out if it hadn't already, and it didn't matter that she hated everything about the situation. There was more at stake than her ego. Her throat tightened. Only it was turning out to be so much harder than she had ever imagined.

Her fingers twitched, and she made a fist, trying to banish the memory of how it had felt when Trip had taken her hand out by the pool. She knew that it had been for Valentina's benefit, oh, and to prove a point, but why then could she still feel the imprint of his touch? Why did it still burn now, sharp and hot like the lick of a flame?

Why then did it make her want more heat? More touch, just more…

Needing to distract herself, she stared through the window at the view. She had been to Rome only once with her parents and she had loved all the art and architecture and the buzz of the moped and the oven-hot streets. But this was the other side to Italy. Lush, rural, so quiet you could hear your heart beating. It was like looking at a painting. Or perhaps the backdrop to a play or a ballet. But there were no dancers waiting nervously in the wings, just horses, heads low as they grazed the lush green grass.

She put down her book.

Her family were sailors. Her dad had a yacht and they spent their summers around Martha's Vineyard, taking the boat out all the way to the Bahamas and back. She liked horses but they were large and unpredictable, so mostly she was happy to look at them from a distance.

But maybe that was something else that was going to have to change too if she was ever going to take a look around her home for the next few days—weeks?—because there seemed to be an awful lot of them.

As if to prove that point, she heard a whinny from nearby and, leaning forward a fraction, she narrowed her gaze in the direction of the sound.

She was more than a little scared of horses, but perhaps if she could get past her fear then everything else would seem easy in comparison. At the very least it would stop her thinking about Trip. First, though, she was going to change clothes. She was just too hot and she couldn't keep wearing the same things day after day.

Having changed into a light gingham print dress with puffed sleeves, which was no doubt her mother's idea of what to wear for some imaginary picnic in the country, she slipped on her sandals and made her way downstairs.

It was easy to find the stables, although only the two-part doors with their hay rails gave any hint that they were for horses, not humans. They shared the same stucco walls and pantiled roof as the main house and were easily the most opulent-looking stables she had ever seen. But there were no horses.

And then she heard it again, the same noise as before, only softer, more of a nickering sound than a whinny. It was coming from a slightly larger building next door, some kind of barn by the looks of it.

The door was shut but it opened easily and she slipped inside, glancing up, momentarily transfixed by the dust motes spiralling lazily down from the ceiling.

And then she saw him.

Trip was standing next to a beautiful chestnut-coloured horse. Given that he was standing in a barn, she would have expected him to be wearing chinos or jeans, but he was still wearing his swim shorts. His one concession to the equestrian setting was that he no longer had bare feet. Instead he was wearing some of those short riding boots.

At first she thought he was on the phone. His head was lowered slightly and one hand was pressing against the side of his face, but then he moved and she saw that it was empty. He seemed to be just standing there. No, not just standing, she thought, her gaze resting on the rise and fall of his chest. He was concentrating.

Abruptly, the horse shook his head and took a couple of steps forward and she saw Trip frown, adjust his breathing, then follow the horse.

Her own breath was trapped in her throat. What was he doing?

Now, Trip was bowing his head again, closing his eyes and for a moment nothing happened and then the horse turned and gently nuzzled his shoulders, and she had a sudden, strong feeling that she was intruding.

Without turning, she took a step backwards and collided with something hard and metallic. A shovel—

'Ouch!'

'Lily?'

The horse made an accusatory whickering sound, but it was Trip's voice that made her legs momentarily weave beneath her, then freeze.

Trip had turned and was walking towards her. In the soft, smothered light of the barn his beauty transcended any words she could muster.

'Are you okay?' He was squinting but she felt his gaze like a searchlight. Behind him, the horse was walking over to tug at a net of hay.

'I'm fine.' She cleared her throat. 'I heard the horses, so I thought I'd come and have a look at them.' Remembering how Trip had followed it around, she said, 'Is it okay?'

'Acrux?' He turned to where the horse was pulling at

the hay. 'He's good.' She couldn't see his face but there was something odd about his voice. A hesitancy, almost as if it was a struggle to speak.

'He's beautiful.'

Another hesitation but the tension in his voice dropped a notch. 'And he's smart. People think horses are just dumb animals, but they're not.'

'Is that why you chose him? His intelligence?'

His face softened. 'I didn't choose him. I bred him, raised him from a foal.'

That surprised her. That he could have that focus and perseverance. Something of what she was thinking must have shown on her face, because his mouth curved up at one corner. 'You don't believe me.'

'Well, it does seem a little out of character,' she admitted. But then it wasn't the first time he'd caught her off guard. Her body stiffened as she remembered the moment when she'd realised that she'd forgotten to upload her speech.

'I never thanked you,' she said slowly. 'For what you did that night at the auction. Stepping in and just giving a speech like that, it was really impressive. I don't know what I would have done if you hadn't been there, so thank you for that.'

There was a short, slightly startled silence.

'What made you think of that?' he said finally.

She shrugged. 'I don't know. Just you being different from how I thought. From how you were when we had lunch that first time.'

He laughed then, a real laugh, not a mocking one, and she couldn't stop her eyes from moving towards the sound. It made her feel as if her limbs were filling with a golden light that poured straight from the sun.

'Yeah, well, that wasn't my finest hour.' His eyes moved to find hers. 'You were pretty impressive though. Seriously bossy, but impressive. I can remember being astonished that you were so young.'

'To be fair, I'd been working on it for some time.'

He shook his head. 'Which is why it was so impressive. It didn't feel like you were phoning it in. You made it feel fresh, exciting. Even though you hated me,' he added.

She felt herself blushing. 'I didn't hate you. Well, maybe I did, a bit, but you were late. And hungover. And distracted.' Her mouth twitched. 'But when I took away your phone, you had a lot of good ideas.'

His eyes were clear and steady on her face. 'We were a good team. And you did thank me that night,' he added softly and there were no words to describe how the softness in his voice made her feel.

Maybe that was why she forgot for a moment why she was there in Italy. Why it suddenly felt as if it were just two people, talking normally, a couple almost. Instead of what they were, which was actors rehearsing their lines for the opening night.

She took a breath. 'I don't know how to do this, Trip,' she said quietly.

His face stilled then and for a fraction of a second, the doubt and nervousness she was feeling was visible in his eyes. And then it was gone. 'You're overthinking it. We're both in the public eye, Lily. Which means having to play a part sometimes, putting on a mask.'

She felt a jolt of surprise. She didn't just wear a mask in public, she wore full body armour. It was the only way she could do the job she loved, be the daughter she wanted to be. But she was surprised that Trip felt that way.

'Remember how we stood up at that auction together.' He was impatient again now. 'It'll be just the same as that.'

Except it wouldn't be, she thought. At home, with her family, her close friends, she was herself, but here with Trip, she wouldn't be able to relax. She couldn't risk letting her guard down and something happening, as it had at her apartment.

'No, it's not. You have live-in staff on site. That means I'll have to be in character almost all of the time.'

His face hardened. 'What do you want me to say, Lily? Life's not fair.'

Lily stared at him, her throat tightening. She didn't need Trip to tell her that it was dog eat dog out there. She knew life wasn't fair.

'Okay, maybe that's the wrong word—'

It was. Expecting her to fake what had once been real was not just unfair, it was unkind.

He cut across her. 'I don't know why you're making it into such a big deal. It's not as if I'm asking you to do something you weren't already willing to do.'

Her heart contracted.

'Yes, you are. We were having sex. In private. Now you're asking me to be your fiancée, your cheerleader, your guarantor. In public.'

He stared at her, his mouth curving upwards into a

shape that was more sneer than smile. She felt her heart thud too hard inside her chest. 'But I'm not asking you, am I?' Now his face was dark with impatience. 'Look, Lily, you know how the world works. People love a story. All we have to do is make them believe it. And you're a very smart woman, so I don't think that's going to be a problem. Particularly as you have an incentive. We both do.'

She drew a rough breath. 'I don't like that word.'

'Which one? Story? Incentive?'

'We,' she said tersely. 'There is you and there is me. We implies consent and intimacy, neither of which are present in this current arrangement.'

His gaze narrowed, mouth curving mockingly. 'You mean current as in this particular moment, because not long ago we were kissing, and it was definitely consensual—'

She could feel the buttons of her dress burning into her skin. The air around them was growing thicker. It was making her breathing go messy and her brain felt fuzzy.

'That was—'

'What?' He raised an eyebrow. 'A bad idea? A mistake?' He took a step forward and she felt the tension between them snap tight as his eyes fixed on where she could feel her nipples pushing against the checked cotton.

'You're lying to me, you're lying to yourself. You wanted me, Lily, you still do. I don't know why you won't admit it—'

He was standing so close she could see the smattering of freckles along his cheekbones, the faint shadow of stubble on his jawline. Too close. But she didn't need to be that close to feel the truth of his words and even though she didn't want them to, they did something to her, made her remember how it felt to see him aroused, to know that she had the power to arouse him.

And right now that felt like the only power she had left.

'So let's have sex.' She took a step forwards, hands on hips as if she were a prizefighter throwing down a challenge. 'Let's do it. Here. Now. Let's have sex here in this barn.'

He looked taken aback in about five different ways, and after so many weeks of feeling conflicted and helpless that felt good.

'What? You said it yourself. I want you, you want me. It's just bodies, and it's not as if we can have sex with anyone else. It might as well be here as anywhere else.'

She reached for him, her fingers clumsy against his shirt, pulling him closer, and she felt him tense, his hands moving to her hips, steadying her, stopping her—

'What are you doing?' His voice was hoarse but he wasn't pushing her away and she could feel him against her stomach, the hardness of him making her shudder inside and arch against him.

As if he weren't the man she had tried to run from. The man who was blackmailing her, as if she were just heat and need.

'Lily, no, not like this—'

It was the gentleness in his voice that made her stumble backwards and she stared up at him, her face burning, and she knew that she was crying. She didn't feel powerful any more. She had wanted to punish him, to make him hurt as he was hurting her, and she knew only one way to do that, because sex was when she had felt his equal.

Not any more.

She was just a tool, a means to an end.

'If not like this, then how?'

Her face was wet, but she didn't brush the tears away, instead she crossed her arms. 'Like before maybe? Is that how you want it to be? Because that can't happen. Not ever.' Her voice was shaking now. 'Do you think because I'm not beautiful like you that I don't have feelings? That I don't care that—'

She pressed her hand against her mouth. She had said too much. So much more than she wanted him to know.

He looked stunned, his eyes wide and bluer than she had ever seen them.

'Lily—'

But she was already moving, stumbling through the door and out into the sunlight and then she was running, running from the pain in her heart and the pity in his eyes.

CHAPTER SIX

LEANING BACK IN the chair, Trip gazed up at the sky and breathed in deeply. It was another perfect day.

The sun was shining hard but there was a light breeze, just enough to make the heat bearable. He tilted the glass in his hand to his mouth. This wine was perfect, too. Cool, bright and energetic with apricot and peach flavours.

Finally, everything was going according to plan.

He glanced across the table to where Lily should have been sitting.

Lily was cooperating. But only in the same way that a soldier accepted being a prisoner of war. Outwardly passive while privately counting down until the day of their release.

Somehow she had managed to eat breakfast and then lunch without saying more than ten words to him in total, before evaporating without any explanation or excuse. It was annoying as hell, doubly so because he could hardly force her to talk to him so the chances of things being any different at dinner seemed slim at best.

Because Lily didn't want to talk to him. Didn't want to look at him. Didn't want to be around him. Which was why he was drinking alone—always a good look—and she was presumably holed up in her bedroom, no doubt hating him with every fibre of her being.

His shoulders stiffened as he remembered that moment out in the barn when he'd realised she was crying.

Because of him.

He gazed up into the sun, deliberately letting the white light fill his head so that it would block out the image of Lily's face and an ache that was stretching from one temple to the other. But that only made things worse because now he could hear her voice.

Not ever.

The phrase batted back and forth inside his head and his fingers moved automatically to tap the union valley point in the webbing between his thumb and finger.

He still didn't understand what had happened in the barn.

That she had even been there at all had thrown him off balance. She wasn't supposed to have been. In fact, he had only been there because the tension between them was turning to chaos beneath his skin.

A shiver ran across the bare skin of his arm. Turning to find her watching him with Acrux, he'd never felt more vulnerable, more exposed. Aside from his immediate family and the various therapists he'd seen over the years, nobody knew that he had ADHD. Not officially anyway. His teachers had suspected, his friends joked about it, but Henry had always refused to have him labelled. The family name must be protected at all costs.

Remembering how he'd used to catch his father watching him sometimes, Trip felt his spine tense.

He'd lost count of the number of times he'd been told that coping mechanisms could and should involve family members, and maybe if his mother had been less wrapped up in her own affairs then it might have been different. She might have recognised and praised his ingenuity and energy and his ability to talk to anyone. Perhaps if Charlie had been closer in age and not so scared of displeasing Henry, they might have been friends and his brother could have helped him navigate those confusing early years.

But the Winslows were not a family. They were four individuals who shared a surname, some DNA and a portfolio of prime real estate.

He was ten when, finally, he'd been diagnosed and initially it had been a relief to know why he was different from other people, particularly the father he admired but with whom he so often clashed. The downside was that his father had made it his mission to 'fix' him and his relief had evaporated and he'd started to feel like a lab rat. There had been countless assessments, medication tried and abandoned, counselling sessions, techniques to master, some of which helped some of the time. But it wasn't until one of the therapists had suggested equine-assisted psychotherapy that he'd found a way to make sense of the chaos inside his head.

And because his dad was Henry Winslow II, he hadn't just sent him to an accredited therapist. Wherever it was possible, his homes around the globe had been equipped with stables and the all-important horses to fill them. On the face of it, his father had gone above and beyond what any parent could reasonably be expected to do.

But it had always felt like just another double-edged sword in their complicated, combative relationship. Because despite the progress Trip had made, it had never been enough.

Not even when he had proven that he was more than capable of running the business, more capable than Charlie in many ways because out of the two of them he was the one who had taken risks. He had gone out on his own without his father's blessing or guidance. And yes, he had failed initially, but for him failure was part of innovating. He anticipated it, accepted it. His goal was always to fail better right up until the moment he succeeded.

And he had succeeded. Above and beyond what Henry had at the same age.

But still his father had made him wait, had held back anointing him as his successor, and, via those old men back at the office, he was still holding him to account even though he had no right because Henry had not been the perfect man he'd claimed to be.

His eyes moved to where Acrux was standing beneath one of the chestnut trees that stippled the curving green landscape. Discovering his father's hypocrisy was just one of the reasons why he was struggling to stop his thoughts from stampeding like a herd of wild horses.

He felt the skin on his face tighten.

What he hadn't fully acknowledged until yesterday was how much Lily was struggling too.

Reluctantly he returned to that scene in the barn,

those grey eyes of hers resting on his face. Curious, but soft too. As if she understood him. As if she had crept beneath the barriers he'd built between himself and the world.

He couldn't remember anyone looking at him like that. Not even his mother. Alessandra Winslow had been too lost in her own thoughts to have ever really focused on his.

Maybe that was why he'd been caught off guard. Why what had happened next had been so shocking that he'd forgotten his frustration and his anger, that dark consuming fury that he couldn't seem to shift so that it felt as though he'd been furious for almost his whole life. Since before he'd found those letters in his father's things.

He felt his chest tighten. He wasn't a total moron. He knew that there was grief mixed up in that terrible fury. But knowing that hadn't done much to soothe the fury, or staunch the pain, the ache of losing his father, not once, but twice, because that was what it had felt like finding those letters. Reading those impassioned words from Henry's mistress had made him question everything he'd thought he knew about the man who'd raised him.

It had been like an oil spill inside his chest, spreading slowly, coating everything in toxic, impenetrable darkness. And he didn't know what to do with all of those feelings.

But then gazing into Lily's eyes in the barn yesterday, he'd felt the world steady. And something had changed. All the anger and frustration had just disappeared and he'd found himself relaxing. It had seemed so easy, just talking, and then she'd smiled and he hadn't been able to breathe because it had never been like that with anyone.

Only then she'd told him that she didn't know how to do this. As if, to her, being there with him in that sun-soaked barn was an effort.

And even though he was used to being made to feel like an unwanted complication, it had stung. More than stung. Her words had pierced like a blade. His hands balled. He didn't understand or like this feeling of need-ing her to like him. It made him conflicted and out-gunned because to feel anything other than simple lust was so alien. And pointless too because in his family emotions had rarely been expressed. Even his father's disappointment had been carefully tempered.

But there was no one there for him to rail against and that was a different kind of pain, but, in the mo-ment, he had wanted to hurt Lily, so he had pushed her to admit her desire.

He sucked in a breath, body tensing as he pictured Lily in that dress with the sunlight behind her, revealing what lay beneath the checked cotton. That she hadn't known what she was revealing had made it even more erotic.

But she had felt it. Felt the shift in the air, felt that quivering, electric thread between them pull taut so that when she'd reached out and touched his chest it hadn't surprised him. What had surprised him, shocked him, was what she'd said and the way she had said it. Talk-ing about sex as if it was just something functional, a nuts-and-bolts need to be screwed tight with a wrench.

Which it was, he told himself irritably. And he had wanted to respond, wanted to press his mouth against hers and his hand against that maddening indent in the small of her back, wanted to fuse her body with his. Only then he had realised she was crying.

Because of him.

He had stopped it, and then she had changed again, pushing him away, her face small and pale and breakable as if he were a stranger, a threat...

And that wasn't fair because, surely, she knew he would never hurt her. Had in fact been trying to do the right thing.

Only now she was acting as if he was the one who had started it. As if being his wife were some kind of life sentence. He got to his feet abruptly and walked swiftly back into the house and up the stairs. Her door was shut, and for a few half seconds he stared at the bland, knotted wood as if that were her answer and then he knocked.

Silence.

He knocked again, more irritably this time because that was who he was, how he was. But there was still no answer, and his anger reared up, full-blooded and un-thinking, and he twisted the handle and opened the door.

'Why the hell do you have to—?'

He stopped. The bedroom was empty. Frowning, he checked the bathroom and the dressing room. Both empty. Heart pounding against his ribs, he stared wildly around the room, his head filling with static and then his gaze narrowed on the window.

Through the glass, he could see a figure in shorts and some kind of top moving determinedly through the grass, and then the land curved away and she disappeared.

Trip felt his pulse accelerate. Was she running or hiding? No matter, he would find her. Not that he'd ever even pursued a woman before.

But then he'd never wanted to.

Lily was walking fast.

Back in her bedroom she had tried reading but every time she'd focused on the page, her mind would turn blank and, before she could stop herself, she'd be right back where she'd started in the barn with the tiled roof, making a fool of herself.

It had been enough to get her moving quietly through her bedroom door and down the stairs. A glimpse of Trip out on the terrace, wine glass in hard, soaking up the sunshine as if nothing were wrong, had sent her spinning away from the villa and across the green grass like a bowling ball.

She had no idea where she was going but just being on the move made her feel calmer. There were horses grazing on the left-hand side of the paddock so she kept to the right, kept moving.

It was her phone that finally stopped her in her tracks.

'Lily?' Her father's voice was so familiar and yet it was still a shock to hear him.

'Daddy.'

'Do you have time to talk? I know Mom told you how happy we are, but I just wanted to congratulate you in person.' He paused. 'Although you're probably still fuming with us, aren't you? I know you must be because I know how independent you are, but Mom and I just wanted you to have some time with Trip. Private time. That's why you didn't tell us about the engagement, wasn't it? Because you hate the drama that goes hand in hand with being my daughter. But you could have told us, you know,' he added gently. 'We would have kept your secret.'

Her fingers tightened around the phone. What she hated was having to lie to her parents. To know that she had made them liars too. 'Of course I'm not angry. And it wasn't your drama I was worried about.' That at least was true.

Her father laughed.

'He certainly knows how to make an entrance. Looks the part, too. In fact I heard yesterday that somebody wants to make a film of what happened to him. Probably be quite the blockbuster. Your mother would certainly go and see it. She's quite taken with him. I was too, although I was a little surprised. I always thought you'd choose some penniless artist.'

He was trying to make a joke but Lily's chest squeezed tight. That her father imagined she had a choice of potential husbands was almost as heartbreaking as his unquestioning acceptance that Trip had chosen her.

'We did connect through art,' she said quickly. That was true too, although their connection had been very different from their current situation.

'You don't need to explain, darling girl. We're just delighted that you've found someone you love. But I hope he knows how lucky he is, and he is lucky, Lily.'

Suddenly she could hardly breathe, much less speak.

Misery was swelling in her throat. Her parents were so partisan, so blind to her imperfections. They would be heartbroken if they ever found out that Trip had picked her to be his wife solely on the basis that she was the woman least likely to spook the shareholders.

'He does, Daddy.' She cleared her throat. 'I should probably be going—'

'Of course, darling. Now you have fun. Mom sends her love, and Lucas does too.'

Lucas.

As she hung up, she stared down at her brother's sweet face. He was the real reason she was here. The reason she was going to go through with this sham marriage for however long it took. Lucas needed to be left alone. She couldn't take back the past, take back the part she'd played, but she could play her part now.

And there were worse places on the planet to be stuck in limbo, Lily thought as she gazed down at the Tuscan countryside. It felt both epic and lost in time, and, truthfully, if she had come here under any other circumstances she would have been enchanted.

And if this were real. If Trip had really proposed…

If. The shortest, cruellest word in the English language, she thought, body swaying forward in the soft sunlight. She was the stupidest of fools to let herself get caught up in this charade. Because that was what this was. Wasn't it?

For him, yes. But for her…

It was hard being here with him, hard to hate him when he was so close. Harder still when he looked at her as if he wanted to know what she was thinking. Wanted to know her.

But not have sex with her.

She'd been humbled before but what had happened in the barn had been the single most embarrassing thing to happen in her entire life. She could still feel the red blotching her skin. It wasn't just that Trip had rejected her, she had made it slap-in-the-face clear that she knew he would never have proposed to her for real, and that it hurt.

She hadn't wanted to wait around to see the pity in the eyes. She didn't need to. She'd seen it enough times in the past.

The first time she'd realised that she was the ugly duckling in a ballet of swans was when she was seven years old. It had been her mother's thirtieth birthday. Her father had secretly arranged to have a family portrait painted and she and Lucas had been very excited to be in on the surprise. It had been a huge success, one of those memories that families talked about for years afterwards.

But her memory of the moment was different from everyone else's. Staring at the perfectly rendered versions of all of their faces, she had suddenly realised she wasn't beautiful. It had been like a thundercloud breaking over her head.

She'd never raised the subject of her otherness. She hadn't known how because her parents had never treated her differently or made her feel less loved, less valued.

But other people did.

Some did it snidely. Others more openly. She had

learned to deflect, to ignore, to not draw attention to herself, to keep her head down. Which had some positives. She had outperformed all her peers at school, and then in college, and after a few years overseeing her parents' charitable trust she had started her own philanthropic advice platform. Her success hadn't completely stopped the trolls, but she'd been busy doing something she loved.

And then she'd met Trip.

Her eyes stung. There must be something wrong with her. After what had happened with Cameron, she should have kept her distance. There was no need to get involved with another handsome, outwardly charming but inwardly self-serving man. Once bitten, twice shy. Or, in her case, spiky.

But Trip had smoothed out all those prickling insecurities.

He had made her feel hungry, lithe and bright with a need that transformed her from flesh and bones into quicksilver.

He had made her beautiful.

But in many ways sex made you as blind and foolish as love did. That was what she hadn't realised before. On the contrary, she had congratulated herself for keeping things contained with Trip in a way she hadn't managed with Cameron.

Because people like her didn't end up with men like Trip. Not in real life. This sham marriage was all that was on offer.

In New York, the sun always felt harsh but here she liked the soft lick of heat and the tease of the breeze.

She stood for a few moments, breathing deeply, letting the light play across her face and then she took a step forward between the leaf-covered branches, and touched the cluster of dark purple grapes. They felt firm and warm. But, of course, what really mattered was how they tasted, and, tongue tingling, she pulled one loose and lifted it to her mouth…

A shadow fell across her. A bird? No, it was bigger than a bird, and she turned to glare at the cloud that had dared to spoil this most perfect of moments.

She gazed up, hand frozen mid-air, the foliage around her suddenly watery at the edges, her vision shuddering just as if she really were suffering from the migraine she had been pretending to have.

It wasn't a cloud. It was the beautiful chestnut horse she had seen in the barn yesterday. Acrux—was that his name?

Yesterday, she had thought he looked like a rocking horse, but he seemed a lot bigger this time. Probably because he was standing closer to her. Or maybe it was because Trip was sitting on his back, his broad shoulders blocking out the sunlight.

'Try some if you want, but you might be disappointed,' he said, shifting forward slightly on the horse's back so that his face suddenly slammed into focus, all dazzling blue eyes and glossy brown hair and that body, solid and humming with that energy that instantly made everything around him feel hyperreal.

'The berries are smaller than with table grapes and the skins are much thicker so there's a much higher ratio of skin to pulp. So you can eat them, but you have to chew a lot and then spit out the skins and the seeds.'

That he was riding without a saddle or bridle was mind-boggling enough to a non-rider like her, but now she watched, muted by a slideshow of emotions, some contradictory, each more intense than the last, as he dismounted, dropping to the grass with the same smooth grace with which he did everything physical. He removed the rope from the horse's neck and gathered it in one hand.

'We do grow some grapes for the table over here.' As he started to walk away, the horse followed him and, after a moment, she followed too.

'These are Italia Muscat. They mostly grow in Puglia commercially, but my father always likes...' He paused, his eyes leaving hers briefly to scan back to the villa. 'He always *liked* to have table grapes, so when he bought the estate they started growing this variety, too, just for the family. I think they taste like wine before it's bottled.'

She felt her nerve ending twitch as he held out a small bunch of golden-skinned grapes. 'Don't worry. They're seedless so you won't end up in the underworld for half the year,' he added as she hesitated.

Her eyes jolted up to meet his. Trip knew about Persephone and the pomegranates?

'Are you comparing yourself to a Greek god now?'

That smile. The one she knew by heart.

'Just try one. Please,' he said softly, but there was a tension beneath the softness.

She was still working to breathe but now she glanced

up at him, caught off balance by the hook in his voice. It wasn't an olive branch or even a pomegranate, but it was a peace offering…or an attempt at one. And the strangeness of that, of Trip Winslow following her here to broker peace, allowed her to take the grape from his hand and bite into it.

It was sweet and the flesh melted in her mouth so that she had to press her hand beneath her lips to catch the juice.

'Good?' Watching her nod, he seemed to relax a little.

He ate a couple and then held out his hand to Acrux.

She frowned. 'I didn't know horses ate grapes.'

'They love them, which is why I don't normally bring him up here.' His eyes found hers. 'But needs must.'

Needs. The word quivered between them and his gaze felt heavy and hot, like the earth beneath her feet.

The sky felt as if it were pressing down on her head and yet something in his eyes made her feel as if she were being lifted. But that was the trouble with Trip— he made her feel two often contradictory things at once.

She cleared her throat.

'How much wine do you produce here?' It was just something to say. She didn't much care, nor did she expect him to know the answer, but he replied immediately. 'Around five hundred cases. We're what you might call a micro-winery, but we've won awards for our *rosato*. According to Stefano, the vineyard manager, we have high hopes for this year's crop. He dropped by this morning. Apparently, they're days away from harvesting, so you'll get to see it, which is lucky. Although I'm guessing you probably don't feel lucky,' he added after a moment or two.

She stared up at him, her heartbeat jamming her throat.

'It's just I didn't think about that until yesterday. When you got upset.' He frowned. 'And I know that you hate me right now, but I didn't have a choice. You see, I was never a contender.' She could see that his anger was back—no, not anger, she thought a moment later. It was frustration and pain too. He was wrapped in it.

She waited, watched him regain control.

'It was always going to be Charlie and then suddenly it was me and I knew a lot of people had their doubts, but I knew I could make the business work harder, smoother, leaner. Just better. And I did, but then I went to Ecuador and when I got back everyone was freaking out and I had to do something because I couldn't lose control of the company. I couldn't prove them right. Not after everything that I'd—'

He broke off, his gaze scanning across the vines, and she knew from the slight rigidity in his shoulders that he was no longer in Tuscany, but back in Ecuador. Her own body tensed as her brain tried to imagine what it must have been like to face violence and death alone. And if she hadn't been here, he would still be alone, she thought with a jolt.

'I don't hate you,' she said at last. Because she didn't. 'But you do stupid things sometimes.'

Thinking back to that moment when the police car had appeared from nowhere and Lucas' pale, frightened eyes had met hers in the rear-view mirror, she cleared her throat. 'Everyone does. And the reason I'm here is because you were right. There will be other, better times for us to break up. Any point, really, when the world isn't fixated on your return from the jungle.'

Trip was gazing down at her in silence and there was something about the expression on his beautiful face, almost as if he hated hearing her say that. Which made absolutely no sense.

Now he was nodding. 'That's true,' he said after a moment. 'But what's also true is that I'm only here because of you. You're the reason I got out of that jungle alive.'

Trip felt his chest tighten. Lily was staring at him, a small, puzzled furrow between her eyebrows. Her hair was tied neatly at the nape of her neck and she was wearing shorts and a cropped white blouse that seemed to hide everything and yet still hint at what lay beneath in a way that both confused and excited him.

'I don't understand.'

Watching her frown, he felt his hands ball into fists.

He hadn't either. He still didn't, which was why he hadn't told anyone what had happened, what he had seen, why he had planned on never telling anyone. But he found that he wanted to tell Lily.

The memory of it was suddenly clearer and more real than the vines and the earth. 'The guy who was in charge of tying me up drank—I could smell the alcohol on him—and one evening I realised I could get my hands free. I waited until they fell asleep and then I took off the blindfold and I managed to get away.'

He could still remember the fear that one of them

would wake or, worse, shoot him. His heart had felt hot and slippery in his chest and he'd had that same feeling of being in a game so that even though it had been the most intense situation he'd ever been in, it had also felt as if it were happening to someone else.

'How did you know which way to go?' Lily's grey eyes were light like summer storm clouds and, suddenly and overwhelmingly so that it winded him, he wanted to bury himself in their softness.

'I didn't,' he said simply. 'I was just making it up as I went along. One day, I was trying to climb up to the top of this ridge when everything just collapsed under me. That was when I lost my water bottle.'

The memory rolled over him like a cool mist, barely there but still enough to chill him to the bone.

'Everything got a bit harder after that.' Catching sight of her pale, stunned face, he forced his mouth to curve at one corner. 'I was so thirsty and I drank from this pool. I don't know what was in the water but afterwards I could hardly walk. I was shivering so much I kept biting my tongue.'

Backed up against a tree, skin burning, canopy closing in on him, he had offered up a prayer in desperation.

'That's when I saw you. You were wearing a cream dress like the one you wore to that lunch meeting the first time we met, and you held out your hand to me—'

He felt his fingers tighten around the rope in his hand. Even then, he'd known he was hallucinating, that Lily was in New York. But he had still reached out for her hand, stumbling forward, heart slowing with relief as her fingers had closed around his and suddenly he had been blinking into the sunlight.

After so many days of near darkness and delirium, he'd thought he was still hallucinating so that for a moment he hadn't even realised that there were people moving towards him. All he'd cared about was Lily and he'd called out her name but, as the dark foliage had fallen away from him and his eyes had adjusted, she'd disappeared, breaking apart into petals.

He blinked away the image. 'That's how I found the village. Because of you. You were there with me—'

She was gazing up at him, an expression on her face that he didn't understand but that turned his heart into a pinwheel beneath his ribs, and he reached out and touched her cheek, grazing his fingers against the skin.

'I didn't mean to make you cry,' he said hoarsely. 'And I didn't not want you yesterday.'

Did that even make sense? Did it matter if it didn't? It was just words, a collection of sounds that were just a step up from the babbling of a child. It didn't come close to what he meant, to what he was feeling. But there was something taking shape between them, something tentative and precious and fragile, and he was scared that if he tried again, he would get it wrong and that newly formed shimmering thing would burst like a bubble.

Maybe Lily felt the same way because instead of replying she swayed slightly, the movement making her lean into the curve of his hand, and he felt his body react instantly. Hungrily.

Her chin jerked up and round towards the rumble of an engine and he followed the direction of her gaze to where a tractor was cresting the brow of the hill. He swore inwardly as Lily stepped back into the shadow of the vines and the air opened up between them.

'It's just Maurizio. He works here,' he said, unnecessarily, because why else would Maurizio be driving a tractor across his land? But he wasn't thinking straight. Correction: he wasn't thinking at all. His mind was just heat and hunger.

Maurizio must have spotted him, because the tractor came to a stop and suddenly it was silent. Trip watched him climb down from the cab. Maurizio had worked on the estate since he'd left school and was now well past retirement, but after his wife's death he had been so lost, so in need of occupation, that Trip had kept him on.

He turned to Lily to explain all of that but she was moving between the vines in that delicate, precise way of hers. At the dark fringe of woods edging the field, he watched as the trees seemed to move apart a little to receive her and then, in the blink of an eye, she was gone.

Something between loss and panic spiralled up inside him but it took another five minutes before he could extricate himself from the old man. By then Lily had long since disappeared. But he had to look for her.

And he knew he would find her. He could feel every single cell in his body, each breath and beat of his heart arrowing in on her location.

It was cool and light and green in the woods. Heart pounding, he followed one of the twisty paths, picking the wider one when it split in two, only to backtrack a moment later to take the one that was more overgrown. And that was when he saw her.

Lily was standing in the middle of the path, her grey eyes wide in the half-light crisscrossing her face, a flush of pink highlighting her cheekbones.

His pulse jumped. They had looked into each other's eyes a hundred times or more over the last few days but there was something different this time, an intensity, an anticipation that made his mouth dry and his stomach tremble.

It was the single most erotic moment in his life. And he hadn't even touched her.

In the distance he could hear the quiet rumble of the tractor, but here in the woods there was nothing but the sound of insects and his breath rising and falling in time to the pulse beating in her throat.

'You waited for me,' he said hoarsely.

Her gaze fixed on his face. 'You came to find me.'

For a moment, neither of them spoke. He felt as though they were underwater, that he was holding his breath. He could hardly bear to move in case he was hallucinating and then she held out her hand and he walked swiftly towards her. As his fingers found hers, she pulled him away from the path, through the undergrowth into a shaded clearing dotted with tiny yellow and blue flowers.

The air was different now, warm and still and shimmering with light and shadow and the static hiss of anticipation.

His heart stopped beating as she stopped and turned and they stared at one another, palms still pressed together.

'Are you going to tie me up?'

It was as if she'd slapped him. He stared at her, his pulse raging. 'What?'

She gestured wordlessly to the rope still coiled around his other hand.

'Is that what you want me to do?' he said hoarsely.

Her pupils flared. 'Yes. But first I want you to kiss me.'

The rope slithered to the grass at his feet as, breathing unsteadily, he leaned forward to cup her chin and his mouth found hers. They kissed, tasting one another, pushing back and forth, each time a little deeper until she pulled back and turned her head to touch her lips to his hand.

'I want you, Lily.'

He found the band at the base of her neck and he pulled it loose, weaving his fingers through her hair.

'And I want you—'

She leaned into him, grazing her body against his, her mouth maddeningly light now against his mouth and then, as his hands reached for her, she pushed him backwards.

'Watch me undress.'

She kicked off her sandals and began to unbutton her blouse, slowly, deliberately slowly, and he watched, his body pulsing with a hunger that seemed to magnify his heartbeat so that he could feel his pulse throbbing through him.

Suddenly losing patience, he pulled her closer, yanking the blouse apart, tearing the fabric as he tugged it away from her arms. She wasn't wearing a bra and he cupped her breasts in his hands, body hardening as she gasped, and then he lowered his mouth to lick the soft skin there, teasing her nipples until they stood proud from her body.

She pushed him back. 'I said, watch me.' Behind her, the trees shivered in the dappled light as she unbuttoned her shorts and let them slide down her legs to pool around her bare feet.

Now she was wearing only a pair of pale peach-coloured panties.

For a moment he thought he might black out and then, toeing off his shoes, he grabbed her wrist and pulled her closer.

'Now undress me,' he said.

Shaking inside, he let Lily pull his shirt over his head and run her hands over his chest, his stomach, sliding her fingers beneath the waistband of his trousers. He felt her tug down on the zip, grunting as she freed him, and then his body turned to iron as she dropped to her knees and took him in her mouth. His breath shuddered in his throat, and he reached down to slide his hand through her hair. Shock waves of desire were rippling over his skin and he jerked his hips backwards.

'Not like that. Not this time.'

Pushing his trousers and boxer shorts down, he knelt in front of her and, running his hands over her breasts and waist and legs, explored every curve, every inch of skin until finally he slid his fingers inside her. She moaned against his mouth and the sound was gasoline to the fire of his hunger and he tore off her panties, shuddering as she wrapped her legs around his kneeling body and lifted herself against him.

He pushed up and into her, and groaned. She was so slick and hot.

'Lily—' He breathed out her name as she pulled him closer, her hand a small, splayed encouragement at his hip, and now he was pushing into her, moving rhythmically, his breath ragged against her throat as she arched against him and he tensed, thrusting upwards, the grip of her muscles sending him over the edge, his climax colliding against hers like a runaway train hitting the buffers.

CHAPTER SEVEN

LILY PRESSED HER head against Trip's muscular chest, her body shattering around him as his hips jerked against her, each movement breaking her into ever tinier fragments. His hand was tight in her hair and she breathed him in like oxygen.

She had tried to forget how good it was between them, tried to tell herself that she had misremembered the storm of their passion. But she had been lying. Trip was the only man who had ever made her feel so helpless and hungry all at once. His was the only touch that could wrap her in a blaze of desire, turn her inside out and dissolve her into a creature of pure, endless need. A woman, no less.

It had been just like that first time. Like every time in between, and maybe it would always be like this with them. With each of them scraped raw, dazed and aching, shivering with the aftershocks of their encounter and that head-spinning need and longing that stormed through their limbs until it exploded into a firestorm that blinded and burned everything in its path.

But they stayed safe, bodies fused in a painless white heat.

'Lily—' She felt his fingers move and then he was

tipping her face up to his, his blue eyes hot and fierce like the centre of a flame. Her legs were still wrapped around his waist and it was then, gazing down at the place where their bodies were pressed together, that she realised that he was still kneeling, his other hand supporting the weight of her so casually that it made her tremble inside.

'I didn't check. Are you…?'

'Yes. I'm on the pill.'

Something shifted in his face, beneath the surface of the skin, too quick to capture, but he didn't make any attempt to break their embrace and she didn't either. She just wanted to stay there for ever, splintered into a thousand pieces, with his hardness clenched deep inside her, and his heart raging next to hers.

It took a while for her muscles to relax, for her to take a normal breath and even then he still held her close. Finally, he shifted his weight, lifting her up and letting her legs drop from around his waist and laying her down on the warm grass. She watched in quiet wonder as he moved to lie down beside her.

A breeze was lifting the leaves high up the trees and she gazed up at the fluttering sunlight as Trip caressed the palm of her hand, his face relaxed, at peace, whereas she—

It had taken only a few minutes but the events of moments earlier were starting to fill her head, each frame tossing up one question after another.

Her eyes moved across the clearing. In this circle of quivering pines and oak saplings it felt as if the world outside were gone, had become a shimmering desert. All that remained was this tiny oasis.

And she had taken his hand and led him here.

What had she been thinking?

Nothing.

She hadn't been thinking, just feeling. Her need to touch Trip, to press up against the familiar curve of his shoulder and the solid warmth of his arms, had spread white and blinding across her mind, blotting out both common sense and any thought of self-preservation.

And she still wasn't thinking about her own well-being now. How could she after everything Trip had been through?

Her fingers moved to touch a long thin scar on his leg and, now that she was looking, she could see more scratches, grazes and discoloured skin beneath his tan.

The creases around his eyes made her heart contract. He was never more beautiful than when he smiled, and the thought of him being hunted, hurt, shot or worse made her feel panicked. She reached up and clasped his face in her hands and pressed a desperate kiss to his mouth, needing to feel his breath, his heartbeat, to prove that he was real.

He kissed her back, his hand moving, his touch firm, compelling, sliding slowly up to cup her breast, palms grazing her already taut nipple, shaping her ribs, her waist, her hips.

She pulled him closer, her breath suddenly staccato in her throat as he lowered his body onto hers and she felt the press of his erection, hard and as thick as her wrist. Helplessly she arched up against him, opening her legs wider, and then he slid inside her and she moaned softly, her pulse frantic against his skin, meeting each thrust of his hips with one of her own until there was nothing but heat and need and their quickening breath.

The sun was starting its downward descent when they finally headed back to the villa. Valentina was in the kitchen, preparing the evening meal. She turned towards Lily and smiled warmly.

'Did you have a nice afternoon?'

Lily nodded. 'We did. We...' She hesitated, dry-mouthed as the events of the afternoon unfurled in front of her eyes in all their naked, unfiltered glory so that she could almost feel Trip's hands on her belly and waist, his fingers light against her hips and between her thighs. She was hardly going to share that version of events with the housekeeper, but she was a terrible liar, particularly when put on the spot like this.

'We—'

'Yes, we did.' Trip cut across her smoothly. 'I showed Lily around the vineyards and then we went for a walk in the woods. To cool off,' he added, his eyes finding Lily's. The slide of blue heat across her skin made her shake inside.

'Do you think she guessed?' Lily asked as they made their way upstairs. 'That we weren't—I mean, that we were—'

Trip's eyebrows pulled together a fraction. 'What? That we were having al fresco sex?' Shaking his head, he reached out and picked some grass seeds from her hair. 'I'm going to go with no. But even if she did, so what? We're engaged. We're allowed to have sex.'

They had reached her bedroom now and he followed her through the door quite naturally, almost as if they were the couple they were pretending to be.

And could be for real?

The romantic part of her that she had always suppressed, or, rather, smothered after the mess she had made with Cameron, unfurled a little and she felt the world rearrange itself into a place of possibilities. In this new world, Trip would tell her that they no longer needed to pretend that they were engaged. That a year wasn't long enough because he wanted to spend the rest of his life with her.

Abruptly Trip leaned forward and wrapped his hand around her head and kissed her hard.

He straightened then, his fingers still tangled in her hair. 'You worry too much. Do you want to take a shower before we eat? Because I'd be happy to join you—'

'No—' She shook her head, the word rushing out to cover how her body had stiffened at his suggestion. Her body was still rippling from his touch. The last thing she needed was to be up close and personal with a naked Trip rubbing soap over her.

'I'll have one later. But I might just go and sort out my hair.'

'Why?' She felt another seismic shimmer ripple across the room as he dropped down onto the bed and stretched out his legs. 'I like it like that.' That remark, or maybe the slow, assessing gaze that accompanied it, followed the suggestion about sharing a shower to press against a point low down in her pelvis.

'It'll get all knotty if I don't brush it through,' she said quickly. 'I can meet you downstairs.'

Inside the bathroom Lily closed the door and leaned against the wood. If only she could go downstairs and climb into the refrigerator, let the chilled air cool the smouldering flame Trip had lit inside her. Because that was the trouble when you played with matches in a heat-wave—you started a fire and there was no water to put it out.

Pushing away from the door, she walked over to the sink, giving the mirror a perfunctory glance as she leaned forward to switch on the tap.

She felt the skin on her back prickle.

As she gazed at her reflection, her cheeks grew hot. It had taken a long time but, after they had finally broken apart that last time, Trip had helped her get dressed. But his mouth had kept finding hers so that she hadn't really been paying much attention and now she saw that, not only were some of the buttons on her top in the wrong holes, but others had simply disappeared.

The heat in her cheeks intensified as she remembered Trip ripping open her blouse.

In that moment she had simply wanted him. Even afterwards as they had lain with their bodies overlapping, she hadn't thought of what came next. Neither, she was sure, had Trip. But for him, the past, their past, was not so very different from this new arrangement. What was it he'd said?

'We're engaged. We're allowed to have sex.'

And they had. And she had loved every febrile second of it. Only this 'engagement' wasn't real. It was a pretence, so sex was superfluous.

Then again, a year was a long time for a man like Trip not to have sex, she thought dully. She felt oddly fragile then, and exhausted.

But then it was a lot, connecting with him like that, not just physically, but hearing him talk about what had happened in Ecuador. Before, with her anger buffering them, it had been easy to hold back other feelings. Confusing, contradictory feelings that were as reckless as Trip's decision to visit a smuggling route used by drug cartels.

Only out there in the woods, something had changed.

Or maybe *she* had changed. She didn't know if it was the sex or because she understood now how close she had come to losing Trip for ever, but her anger was starting to lose shape, to crack and crumble, and other emotions were starting to seep through.

This engagement couldn't work, *she* couldn't make it work if she let Trip get under her skin. She couldn't change what had happened but that didn't mean it had to happen again.

Even if she wanted it to.

Her fingers pressed against the cool porcelain of the sink.

And she did want that.

She might be lying to the rest of the world, but she couldn't lie to herself, and when he'd leaned over a few moments ago and fitted his mouth to hers, the desire to keep kissing him, to touch his face and press her hand against where she knew his body would be hardening, had been nearly impossible to resist.

And the intensity of that struggle proved to her that she had to stay within the lines because that was the trouble with sex. You had to be intimate, and intimacy combined with hormones fed into that biological need all humans had to be held and touched. But this arrangement was already complicated enough. Casually, carelessly introducing another layer of complexity for something as transitory and self-indulgent as sex had bad idea stamped all over it.

His hand moving against her cheek, the potent blue of his gaze holding her still, captive as his body sank deeper into her in the dappled light...

She blanked her mind.

It didn't matter that it had felt so right and so real and so perfect with Trip, her judgement was flawed. Cam had taught her that, then Trip had hammered it home and she was still living with the collateral damage from both of those miscalculations.

Staring at her reflection head-on, she rebuttoned her top correctly and smoothed her hair back into another low ponytail and, then taking a deep breath, she opened the bathroom door.

Her pulse skipped a beat.

Trip was still lying on the bed. The book she had been trying to read for days now lay open in his lap.

'Ms Lily Jane Dempsey. BA Amherst, MBA Oxon.' Trip shifted against the pillows. 'You have a lot of letters after your name.'

It was then that she realised he was holding out her

invitation to the scholarship reunion dinner she had been using as a bookmark.

'You have them too.' He had been to Harvard.

'True.' She saw something flash across his eyes, too fast to catch, like a fish darting away from an unseen predator in an ocean of blue.

'So did you have fun?' His eyes were clear and blue and fixed on her face as if he cared, which seemed unlikely but today was turning out to be a day where little, if anything, made sense and so she simply shook her head.

'I didn't go. I had a lot on at work,' she lied.

His gaze held hers, jaw tightening infinitesimally. 'And that's the only reason you didn't go? Because of work?'

No, it wasn't. The dinner had taken place the weekend after he'd come and ended things with her and, for days after he'd left her, her body had felt tired and achy as if she'd had flu. But there was no reason to share that with Trip now. No reason to ever share it with him.

'Not completely. I was worried about you.'

'But you wanted to go—'

She nodded. 'I had a great time in England and I made friends there. I don't often get a chance to catch up with them so, yes, I would have gone.'

'Is that why you were going to London? You wanted a trip down memory lane?'

What she had wanted was to get away from him, this man sprawled on her bed, before he could take the wild rapture of their time together and turn it into something ugly. Before he made it so that all she could remember was that he had named her as his fiancée because he thought her dull and sensible enough to reassure his jittery shareholders.

'You mean, the other day when you tricked me into coming here?' She watched that mouth of his flex into something not quite a smile.

'In part. But it's also because England isn't New York. London can be tricky but in Oxford it's not that hard to have a normal life.'

'You mean, no press?'

In short, yes. No press meant no photos, which meant no humiliation, no jeering headlines, no mocking memes.

She shrugged. 'To an outsider, all students look pretty much the same so it's easier to be anonymous.'

'Easier?' He frowned.

'People think they can say things. Because of my father.' She could feel his gaze, curious but a little baffled because, of course, what did he know about being belittled or deemed inferior? 'And I know that how they talk about me, what they say, is because they're angry, and that anger kind of spills out. But sometimes it's hard—'

It had been bliss. For the first time in as long as she could remember she had fitted in seamlessly. And she had loved it. Loved the old stone buildings. The book-lined libraries. The seriousness of it all. She had felt accepted, felt safe.

It was one of the reasons why returning to the US fifteen months later had been such a shock. Suddenly she'd been back in the spotlight for all the wrong reasons. The brutality of it had left her winded, then angry, and angry people were vulnerable to manipulation. Which was why she hadn't seen Cameron Carson for the danger he was. Why she needed to remember how that felt and not let herself get lost in a pair of blue eyes. She couldn't be trusted. More importantly, he couldn't either.

Suddenly she felt close to tears as she made a different, more painful journey down memory lane, back to when she had found Lucas on the floor of his bedroom, the pill bottle beside him. It was her fault that had happened. Blinded by her own neediness, she had placed her trust in someone who was a literal walking, talking red flag.

And this neediness she was feeling now meant that she couldn't trust herself, trust her judgement. In fact, it was a reason to do the polar opposite of what she wanted to do. So there would be no more giving into that hunger that had stormed the barricades of her common sense and self-preservation out there in the woods.

And she would tell Trip that.

But it would be easier to have that conversation when he wasn't lying on her bed as if he were her fiancé for real, rather than an ex she'd had sex with for reasons that frankly had made sense only in the heat of the moment.

Needing space from that thought, from him, she glanced down at her watch.

'Is that the time? We should go down for supper. It's past seven.'

Glancing across the table, Trip licked the spoon clean and rested it in his bowl. Something was different, he thought, his gaze leapfrogging from Lily's shuttered grey eyes to the pulse beating out a staccato rhythm at the base of her throat.

'Was everything okay?'

Valentina had come to clear the table.

'It was delicious. I wonder if I might be able to have the recipe. *Bunet* is my father's favourite dessert.'

Watching Lily smile up at the housekeeper, he felt an unfamiliar pang of envy, both for that smile and the way her eyes softened when she mentioned her father. It was the same, he noticed, whenever any of her family called or texted. Her face, her voice would alter because, despite the part they had played in getting her here, her love for them was clearly unconditional. And they loved her, too, and he felt uncomfortable at having so casually exploited that love.

Uncomfortable too with that hunted look on her face when she talked about people saying things about her, presumably on the Internet. He had no idea what mud they could throw at Lily. She was smart and hard-working and loyal and brave and passionate. Not that she was perfect, he told himself, feeling his body twitch in response to just how passionate Lily could be. She was stubborn and snippy too. But still, he didn't like knowing that she had been picked on in that way.

'Prendiamo il caffè in salotto, per favore,' he said quietly to Valentina, then, pushing back his chair, he turned to Lily. 'Shall we?' It was a question but also an assumption and he took a step back to allow her to pass.

It was four hours since she had taken his hand and led him into that clearing and his body was still flushed with post-orgasm dopamine so that it had taken a little while for him to register it, but at some point between then and her walking out of the bathroom, something had changed.

She had changed.

At first, he'd thought it was just her blouse. She had done up the remaining buttons in their correct order, which was a pity. How Lily looked after sex was one of the things that gave him the greatest pleasure. Ever since that first time, he had loved knowing that he was responsible for her hair tumbling loose over her shoulder. Loved, too, the contrast with how prim and poised she normally looked.

But there was more going on than a few adjustments to her blouse.

On the way back to the villa she had got quieter, and, even though they had been holding hands, he had been able to feel her retreating from him so that every time he'd glanced over at her, she had been a little more out of reach. And now she was so distant and distracted it felt as if she were behind glass.

His eyes rested on the faint red marks on her bare shoulder where, earlier that day, his stubble had scraped against her skin.

And it didn't take a genius to work out what was on her mind.

She looked up at him then, her grey eyes resting on his face then moving past his shoulder as if it hurt her to look at him.

Which was ridiculous, he thought, with a flicker of irritation, given that her body had been fused to his for most of the afternoon.

'Is everything okay?'

'Everything's fine. I think I caught the sun earlier.'

He glanced over at her pale face, his chest tightening. Now she wasn't just holding back, she was lying. And it didn't make any sense that he should mind. This whole arrangement was a web of lies, but that was hard for him too, although he doubted that she'd believe that.

Somewhere in his head he could hear his mother's voice as she made up yet another excuse.

Of course, she had plenty of practice, he thought, his eyes moving past Lily's face to the classical acoustic piano at the other end of the room. His father had often been late or he would change his plans at the last minute. Nothing was sacred. Not anniversaries or school sports day or birthdays.

There were so many to choose from but one in particular stood out. He and his mother had flown to Italy for Spring Break. It had been the weekend of his father's birthday, but Charlie had been studying for his exams and had stayed on at grad school to revise, and Henry Sr had been due to join them but then, inevitably, he had called to say that he would be delayed.

Trip felt his gaze drift back through the house, seeing his eleven-year-old self. He had been out riding all afternoon and come back hungry, and feeling guilty because he had left his mother on her own. But the house had been so quiet that for a moment he'd thought it was empty.

And then he'd heard it. A tiny catch of breath, like a gasp.

She had been sitting at the piano in this very room

and at first he had thought she was singing softly to herself as she had sometimes when it had just been the two of them. Then he'd realised she was crying. Which had been the other, more likely option. But no child wanted to find their mother weeping.

Not that his mother had seemed to realise that. Her face had stiffened but it had been several moments before her hand had risen like a brushstroke to wipe away the tears.

'Everything's fine. It's this melody, it always makes me weep.'

His childish self had accepted her explanation. But then six weeks ago he'd found the letters and the first one he'd picked up had made it clear that his father had been with his mistress that night. Had chosen to be with her instead of his family.

He felt the shock of it reverberate through him as if it had only just happened. For so long he had chased the perfection his father had demanded. But all the time Henry had been presenting a perfect front, he had been lying, cheating, deceiving. And constantly calling his youngest son to account.

The memory of his father's cool, excoriating gaze made his spine stiffen. Or maybe it was that he felt like a hypocrite for getting so out of shape with Lily for lying to him when he'd made her an unwitting and unwilling accomplice to his lies.

His jaw tightened. But her lying to him was different from the two of them deceiving other people. Her lies were personal, and it hurt because, confusingly and without precedence, he found that he cared about what she thought of him.

'Why don't you just say it? Whatever it is that you want to say but aren't.'

His voice was harsh, too harsh. He knew that even before Lily's eyes pulled back to his.

As Lily's forehead creased, he made an impatient sound. 'I'm disappointed, Lily. It's not like you to play dumb. In either sense of the word.'

There wasn't a flicker of reaction on her small, pale face but, as a silence settled between them, her cool grey eyes fixed on his and he saw the truth. She was angry.

'Okay,' she said at last. 'You want to talk about what happened earlier? I don't regret it—'

He shifted back against the cushion, his heartbeat suddenly and unaccountably running wild beneath his ribs because he didn't want to hear the end of her sentence. Didn't want to hear her tell him that it was a mistake. Or worse, imply that he was a mistake.

'That's lucky.' He cut her off. 'Because it's a little late for regrets.'

She blinked as if she were momentarily blinded by the blindingly obvious then. 'But it shouldn't happen again.'

Not happen again? He stared up at her, seeing that moment in the clearing when he'd let the rope drop to his feet, feeling the pulse in her throat leap towards him, each beat, separate and vivid like the first heavy drops of rain from a thundercloud.

'Any particular reason why not?'

'You know why,' she said after a moment, as if she'd

needed a breath or two before she could speak. There was another sliver of silence and then she frowned. 'It's not what I want.'

'Not what you want?' He held her gaze, not seeing her as she was now, pale and stiff and hostile, but as she had been earlier, arching against him beneath the quivering leaves. 'And what do you want me to say to that? Other than I don't believe you.'

Her eyes darkened and a flicker of lightning split the irises. 'I don't want you to say anything. I want you to listen. For once.'

The 'for once' scraped against his skin like a blunt blade.

'I am listening, and you're lying.'

She was shaking her head now. 'Just because someone says something you don't like doesn't mean it's a lie, Trip.' Her jaw jammed out at an angle that made him want to lean in and fit his mouth to hers, and prove her wrong.

'My liking or not liking what you're saying is irrelevant to its veracity, Lily.'

He got to his feet at the same time as she did and now they were inches apart, close enough that he could see her chest rising and falling. See a brightness in her eyes that she wouldn't share with him.

'In other words, you don't care what I want, but then I knew that anyway.' There was a second of silence. 'So what happens now? Are you going to try and manipulate me into thinking your way is the only way?'

He clenched his teeth. 'What the hell are you talking about? Is that who you think I am?' The thought angered and appalled him. Maybe it did her, because her chin jerked up.

'No, I don't but—'

'So why are we arguing about this?'

'Because you make assumptions. Back in New York you assumed I'd just go along with what you wanted, what you needed, never mind what I felt, and then when that didn't work you brought me here and assumed I'd give in. And now you're assuming that because we had sex, it's going to happen again.'

He held her gaze.

'I was assuming it would happen again because we both enjoyed it. Or are you going to lie about that too?'

That caught her off balance. She swayed a little as if she was going to fall into his arms but then her body stiffened.

'No, I'm not going to lie about that.'

There was a shake to her voice that made the air hiss at the edge of the room. 'I did enjoy it, and I know it felt like it did before and if we had sex again, it would probably feel the same way. But it's not the same. None of this is real. Acting like we can just pick up where we left off will just complicate things, and it's not fair of you to assume that can happen. Because it can't. Because back then we were honest about what we wanted, and I don't want to take that truth and mix it up with all these lies.'

'It's not all lies—' he protested.

'You're not that man that I waited for after the auction, and I can't pretend you're him—'

He tried to set his face to blank as he had done so many times in the past, but it felt as though he were

dissolving. But why should he be surprised? Even before he'd lost his whole family, there had been nothing
solid in his life. Not as Lily had. No core of love and
understanding and acceptance. The nearest he'd got to
it was Mason Cooper, who had at least sat him down
and talked to him.

But Lily had listened. Talking to her earlier about
what had happened in the jungle, he had felt as if he
could tell her anything, felt as if she cared, so that just
for a moment he'd forgotten that this was supposed to
be a charade for the shareholders.

He had to clear his throat to speak. 'It gets easier with
practice.' His mouth twisted into an approximation of a
smile. 'You know, all my life I've been the runner-up,
but this is the first time I've come second to myself.'

Lily watched him turn and walk away, her head still
trying to make sense of the expression that had skid-
ded across his face. Not anger this time, but pain, and
a kind of exhaustion.

The room felt cold all of a sudden. Her heart was
beating crazily fast, as if she had been sprinting for a
finish line, and she had in a way. Only now the prize-
winner's medal looked cheap and tarnished.

What had he meant, saying he was always the runner-
up? It made no sense. Trip had everything. Looks, charm,
brains, money…

And yet there had been an emptiness to his voice
that was as baffling as his words. She glanced furtively
across the room towards him. A lock of hair had fallen
half into his eyes and he blew it away in a gesture that

was so unselfconscious and familiar that she had to look away. It would be so easy to give into temptation, and Trip was the definition of temptation. But she had been tempted before by another not quite so beautiful or charming man and look at how that had ended.

Not with any attempt to explain his behaviour, she thought, replaying Trip's words from earlier.

On legs that shook slightly, she walked over to where he was sitting on the piano stool, his fingers splayed above the polished ivory keys.

Her heart was beating with clumsy little jerks.

'I didn't know you could play,' she said quietly as he raised his head.

'I can play a bit. Charlie was the musical one. I think he could have been a professional, but he was already lined up to take over the business.' There was that same depth of loss to his voice and she shivered, imagining a world without a brother. How close she had come to that happening.

'He seemed kind.'

Charlie Winslow had lacked the precision-cut features and seductive, curling mouth that made Trip shift the gravity in any room, but she could still remember him and she wondered what kind of hole his death had left in his younger brother's life.

'You never said you knew him.'

'I didn't know him. But I dropped my ice cream once at a polo match and he went and bought me another one.'

Trip nodded slowly as if picturing the scene. 'He was a good son. A good guy, I think,' he added. 'We weren't close. He was much older than me.' A catch of breath lifted his chest and she felt her ribs squeeze around her heart.

'It was supposed to be him running the business.' His gaze dropped to his hands. 'I'm just the understudy. Or that's how my father saw me.'

The air in the room seemed to gather and tense. She stared at him uncertainly. 'You were running the Far East division of one of the biggest corporations in the world,' she said finally. 'That's hardly being an understudy.'

Trip turned his head. There was that same exhaustion on his face as before, but now it was tinged with a self-mockery that pulled at her. 'My father liked that my company was touted as a unicorn, so he invited me into the family business. But we never really saw eye to eye. I found his management style too constrictive and cautious.' He reached out and pressed two keys down together to make a jarring, discordant sound. 'And, well... I wasn't exactly what he had in mind for a son.'

Was that true? She realised she and Henry had discussed his wife a couple of times and he had mentioned Charlie in passing, but he had never once mentioned his younger son.

Trip had turned away and had begun to play the opening bars of an aria she recognised. He was wrong, she thought, gazing at his profile. He could play, and more than a bit. And he must be wrong about his father, too, but she couldn't think of a way to say that without sounding either patronising or dismissive.

'You don't believe me.' He straightened then, blue eyes narrowing on her face.

She shook her head. 'It's not that I don't believe you. I just don't understand why you would think that.'

'Join the queue,' he said with a smile that contradicted the edge to his voice. 'Nobody understands anything I think or do. My incomprehensibility is part of who I am. You see, I have letters after my name too—'

Was he talking academically? 'I know.' She frowned. 'You went to Harvard—'

'I never got my degree. I didn't finish. I dropped out.' That note in his voice was one she had heard so many times before—mocking, careless, with a shadow underneath that made his face seem older, wary and weary.

He took a long breath and she watched his profile tighten. 'My letters aren't like yours. Or Charlie's. And my father hated it because he couldn't change them, and because he couldn't change them, he ignored them.'

There was a taut, humming silence.

'What letters?' she said quietly.

He hesitated then, and for so long that she thought he had unilaterally ended the conversation but then, finally, almost imperceptibly, his shoulders shifted.

'ADHD. I'm sure you've heard of it.'

She felt as if he'd slapped her across the face. 'I—I didn't know—' But how? How could she not have known? She felt confused and ashamed.

'Outside the family and a couple of therapists nobody does officially. My father didn't want me to have a label. But I didn't need one anyway. He made it clear that I wasn't ever going to be good enough.'

The ache in his voice made her feel as though she were turning to stone. She had been so sure before that she knew who Trip was. Had readily accepted, in fact, that he was like Cameron. A beautiful, but unscrupulous, self-serving charmer. It was why she had kept her distance, kept it strictly physical. But this man was more than a pretty face. He had been hurt, badly, been judged and found wanting, and she understood how that felt. Only it was worse for Trip because her critics were strangers. His were people who should have loved him unconditionally.

Her chest was so tight now it was hard to breathe. She knew how hard it was to trust, how hard it must have been for him to talk about himself. But he had trusted her.

Glancing up at him, she saw that the last rays of sun were flooding through the window, blazing so brightly that he seemed to be losing shape, and she felt a rush of panic that he would dissolve into the light just as he had disappeared into the darkness of the rainforest.

'When did you get diagnosed?'

'When I was about ten, but I think my mom suspected way before that. My teachers, too. But my dad didn't want to hear it, and besides, he had Charlie, and Charlie was always first and top.'

His mouth twisted into a shape that made her breath catch in her throat.

'You know, I think it killed him that we shared a name. It's probably why I was always "Trip". And because, deep down, I think he thought it suited me. He was always so precise, so absolute and I was impulsive, reckless, a risk-taker so sometimes I'd trip or stumble.'

She reached out and covered his fingers with her

hand. 'We all stumble sometimes.' And sometimes you ran into the spears and arrows willingly, stupidly, selfishly, she thought, remembering Cameron's sly smile. 'And when you set your mind on something, you make it happen.'

He raised an eyebrow. 'You mean like abducting my ex?'

Her fingers tightened around his. 'Actually, I was thinking about your company. Nobody builds a unicorn business by luck. You need expertise, drive, optimism, an understanding of the customer and the market.' She hesitated. 'And I'm not your ex. You're stuck with me, remember?'

'I wanted to be, remember?' he said, his gaze moving over her in that way he had that made everything inside her feel sweet and slow-moving.

She bit her lip. 'Are you on medication?'

'Not any more. I was when I was younger, but some of my symptoms stopped when I got older and some of them I manage with coping strategies and therapy.'

'Like tapping?'

He nodded. 'Tapping and CBT.' Turning her hand over, he stared down at it as if he was making up his mind about something. 'And natural lifemanship. That's where you work with horses to regulate your body's energy. I'd always ridden and one of my therapists mentioned it to my mother. I tried it and it really clicked with me.'

So that was what she had seen in the barn.

'How does it work?' she asked.

'It helps develop your understanding of non-verbal

cues. You see, horses are highly selective about who they trust so you have to learn how to control the chaos inside. That helps you deal with what you see as the chaos around you.'

She could see him standing, head bowed, trying to steady his breathing. 'Is that why Acrux walked away from you?'

He nodded slowly. 'After we argued, I was spinning out. Angry with you. Angry with myself too. He could feel it…' His voice trailed off and she could feel his regret pulling at her like a tide. 'I'm sorry, Lily, for making this your problem. For making assumptions and for lying to you. And your parents.'

He was apologising? Staring down at him, she felt that same quiver of petals opening in spring sunshine. Trip had hurt and manipulated her and the closeness of his behaviour to Cameron's had struck a still raw nerve. But they were not the same. She knew that now.

'I was angry with you too.'

'You had every right to be. You still do.' He made a small, tense gesture with his other hand. 'I've messed everything up. I thought it would be easy, but I don't know how to do this either. But I do know I can't do it on my own.'

'You're not on your own. We're in this together,' she said, suddenly fierce.

His blue eyes locked with hers and she stared up at him, mesmerised, thrilled almost by the expression on his beautiful face, as if they really were together.

'I think you mean that.'

'I do,' she said, and it was hard to hear her voice over the clattering of her heart.

He touched her cheek near the hairline. 'You were right earlier. About me. I did make assumptions. About what would happen. Because I'm used to people falling in line with my wishes. But also because I wanted you. Always. Right from that lunch meeting when you gave me such a hard time.

'I know I've hurt you, and I regret that more than anything, but I can't regret bringing you here, Lily.'

The softness in his voice made her name sound like a poem and she wanted to bury her face in the crook of his neck.

'I can't regret being with you, being inside you, because it's real. What happened in that wood was real. And what we have together is the simplest, realest part of me.'

It was too much of a risk to tell him she felt the same way. It would be an act of wanton recklessness and she opened her mouth to tell him that nothing had changed. That what happened in the wood should never happen again. But she couldn't somehow. It was as if something had changed between them. It wasn't only the sex. It wasn't even his apology.

It was him. And she didn't want to think about what that meant. She just didn't want to lie to him.

'For me, too,' she whispered, and his pupils flared, and when he slid his hand along her cheek she leaned into it and then he was pulling her against him and his mouth found hers and he took, and took and kept taking as the light turned to darkness around them.

CHAPTER EIGHT

'*GRAZIE*, VALENTINA. I've got it from here.'

Smiling easily at the housekeeper, Trip closed the door. He deposited the tray on the chest of drawers and then picked up the remote control and watched the curtains slide apart fractionally.

It was morning, and outside it was looking as though it was going to be another perfect day of clear blue sky and bright sunlight, made all the more perfect because Lily was in his bed, her long hair fanned out against the pillow, her eyelashes fluttering in her sleep.

He gazed down at her small oval face.

He still couldn't quite believe that she was here. But when, finally, they had stopped kissing, she had taken his hand and led him through the house and up the stairs as if it were something they did every night. On the top step, she had turned to him, her pupils flaring as he'd stared down at her, and without speaking, without needing to speak, he had scooped her into his arms and carried her to his room.

Not to sleep. His body tensed, remembering the splay of her limbs against the white linen and the curve of her throat arching beneath his lips.

It had felt like a miracle so that he had been buzzing, but in a good way. All the tension and obstacles of the last few weeks dissolving into the certainty of their desire, so that, waking this morning, he had felt smooth and ironed out in the way that only sex with Lily could make him feel.

But that had all come later.

Before, while he had still been reeling from that feverish encounter beneath the trees, she had told him that what had happened in the woods was a one-off, not quite a mistake but a misstep, and it had punched a hollow in his chest, just like when he had found those letters. There was that same feeling of powerlessness and panic, and he'd had to walk away. Only he hadn't got as far as Ecuador this time.

And it wasn't a phantom Lily who had come to find him.

His chest felt tight or full, as if something were pushing against the ribs.

She was real, and this time when she'd taken his hand, she had led him out of the jungle inside his head, where instead of twisted tree roots and slippery rain-soaked ground there had been dark, tangled memories bookended by that expression on his father's face.

He still wasn't entirely sure why he had opened up to her. Or why it hadn't been the sky-falling-in-on-his-head moment that he had imagined it would be, because somehow, despite everything he had done to her, Lily had made it easy for him to talk about himself, about the diagnosis that he had kept hidden for so many years.

She had listened in that careful way of hers and asked

some questions, but she hadn't tried to make out ADHD was a superpower or that it was something that needed fixing.

She had simply accepted it. Accepted him.

Chosen him.

An unfamiliar feeling pulsed across his skin, vivid, blazing gold and, suddenly needing to reassure himself that she still felt that way, he reached out to stroke her face. She shifted in her sleep, eyes blinking open, and he felt his body tense, nervous suddenly that the sunlight beating through the window would break the spell that had brought her to his bed. But then she gave him a small, sleepy smile.

'Hi.'

'Hey,' he said softly as she looked up at him. 'I hope you're hungry. I had Valentina bring up some breakfast.'

The pastries were delicious, buttery and still warm from the oven and Lily ate appreciatively and with an appetite that surprised her. For weeks now it had been a struggle to eat anything, but all those knots in her stomach had simply disappeared.

Trip seemed easier too. There was still that pulsing energy humming beneath the golden skin, but the edginess that had seemed to cling to him like a shadow was gone.

And it wasn't just that release of tension that followed sex.

It was as if something deep inside him had shifted, unlocked, opened. But then he had opened up to her, she thought, remembering last night's revelation. She glanced over to where he was lounging on his side, his head propped up on his elbow, one finger chasing flakes of laminated pastry around his plate.

Not that she saw Trip as in any way defined by his ADHD. It would take so much more than four little letters to sum up the man in front of her. But it made sense of that fizzing energy and force that seemed to radiate from him. And there were other things too that were probably explained by the neurological make-up of his brain, like his impulsiveness and those sudden bursts of intense focus.

It was a part of who he was, like Lucas' ability to hear music inside his head, and she could no more imagine Trip being any other way than she could envision the ordeal he'd had in the jungle.

And what had she done? Nothing. Not a thing. She had sat and stared at the news bulletins. But it was as though her head had been filled with mist. Everything had been muffled, except her own voice inside her head telling Trip that she wouldn't care if he never came back from Ecuador.

Those words had haunted her for weeks.

'I shouldn't have said what I said when you left. About not bothering to come back. I never wanted that, but you hurt me and I wanted to hurt you. So I said things that weren't true.'

'You said a lot of things that were true too.' Now he stretched out a hand and took hold of her wrist. 'I was selfish that day, and thoughtless and I hurt you and I hate that I did that. I wish more than anything that I hadn't done it—'

He meant the way he'd ended things, she told herself quickly, not *that* he'd ended things. Although it would be so tempting to think that was what he wished when his eyes were holding her captive and there was no distance between them any more.

'I wish I could change things, change the past—'

She could hear the regret in his voice, and another note she couldn't quite put her finger on. But she understood only too well the anguish of remorse and wishing to have done things differently.

'Not all the past,' she said quietly.

Her skin tingled as he looked at her for another long moment. 'You're a good person, Lily.'

She glanced past him to the clock by the bed. It was Tuesday morning in New York. The second Tuesday of the month. Lucas would be talking to his therapist. Picturing him, scrunched up in a chair, she felt the crushing weight of her guilt. She wasn't a good person at all, but, unlike Trip, her failings were not in the public domain because her father had used his influence to make the mess she had made shrink to the point where the consequences of her actions amounted to little more than a talking-to.

'Too good for me,' Trip continued. 'And I know I messed up your plans, so I'd like to make it up to you.'

'And how are you planning on doing that?'

Her abdomen tensed as he leaned forward and kissed her shoulder.

'I have an idea. But I'm open to suggestions.' She heard the smile in his voice and when he lifted his face, she saw that his eyes were bright with a heat that she could feel inside.

'Let me hear your idea first,' she said quickly, shivering as he bent his head and kissed the side of her throat.

'I thought I might take you to England.'

'England?' His mouth was moving lower and she was finding it increasingly difficult to form sentences.

'We could fly there today. You could show me around Oxford. I know how much you wanted to go, and I want to take you. Would you let me do that, Lily? Would you let me do what I want?'

He was sliding down the bed and now she felt his warm breath above the cluster of curls between her thighs.

'Yes,' she said hoarsely, and then he was parting her legs and she arched against his mouth and she couldn't speak, couldn't think because her mind was nothing but heat and hunger.

They arrived in Oxford the following morning.

After the open hills of Tuscany, the city felt hot and airless.

'I forgot how many tourists there are in the summer,' Lily said, gazing out of the window of the car at the people crowding on the pavement.

'We'll fit right in, then.' Trip pushed back his fringe and pulled a ball cap onto his head. 'We have a map too.'

She laughed as he produced it with a magician's flourish. 'I don't need a map. I lived here for over a year.'

'I know but it's part of our disguise.' He gave her one of those megawatt smiles then and she felt her heart contract. It would take more than a map and a ball cap to make Trip disappear into the crowd.

'*Our* disguise?'

'You have a cap too.'

The blue of his eyes was glossy and sharp and she was touched by how much thought he'd given to their visit. 'Did Lazlo get these?'

That smile.

Trip was a member of the Diamond Club, and Lazlo, the club's concierge, had quietly and efficiently arranged everything, including conjuring up a private jet, a car complete with driver and security detail, and a discreet, fully staffed home for the entirety of their stay. But then it was probably a work of moments for the man who had got Trip out of Ecuador and back to New York without so much as one news story breaking.

'There's nothing he can't get hold of. That's why he was the first person I called in Ecuador when I got to the village. He had a car there within an hour. But that's kind of the point of the club. Their concierge service doesn't just do your laundry, it can facilitate things. Legally, of course. Well, mostly,' he added, and she felt her skin tighten as his smile reached his eyes. 'Ah, we're here.'

'Is this it?' Lily gazed up at the honey stone, three-storey town house. 'I cycled past here every day on my way to college. I used to wonder who lived here.'

'We do.' Trip nudged her out of the car. 'For the next few days anyway.'

The house was cool and elegant inside, but it was the

views across the sun-soaked city that excited her most. If she stood on tiptoe she could just see Magdalen Tower.

'Is it okay?'

'It's perfect.'

Trip was standing behind her now. 'So, what do you want to do first?'

Her pulse gave a twitch.

'This,' she said softly and, turning, she leaned in and kissed his mouth, her body turning to flame as he pulled her closer.

It was early afternoon before they finally left the house. A sudden short downpour had emptied the streets and left the city gleaming in the returning sunlight. They wandered slowly, enjoying the languid heat and their lack of purpose, moving closer to one another as other tourists gradually emerged from shops and cafes to join them.

'Impressive,' Trip said, turning on the spot. 'So this is your old college. We should get a photo.'

'No, honestly, we don't need to—' she protested, but it was too late. Trip was already pulling her against him and holding up his phone.

With an effort, she tried to paste a smile onto her face. Over the years, and thanks to the numerous staged family photos required by a US senator, she had learned how to pose for the cameras, but she still found it hard not to stiffen. And even harder not to snatch the phone out of his hand, because photos were so unforgiving, and selfies were the most brutal of all. There was no softening at the edges. Every flaw was there in close-up.

And he would see it, and then she would see his pity…
She grabbed the phone.

'Hey—' Trip turned towards her, laughing, thinking she was messing around, and then his smile fell away, his eyes narrowing, and she knew that her face must be as tense and panicky as she felt. He hesitated, then took her hand, the one not holding his phone, and it was only when he began to gently open her fingers that she realised her fists were clenched.

'What is it?' And then when she didn't reply. 'It's just me taking a photo. What's the worst that could happen?'

She stared at him, her pulse jerking in her throat.

'It doesn't matter. I want to go back to the house—'

She felt light-headed, the misery in her chest suffocating her, but then she felt his arm slide around her waist, warm and solid, and he was steering her away from the crowds, leading her quietly and calmly across cobblestones into a park, where everything was quiet and green like the woods in Tuscany where he had come to find her, to hold her against him.

As he sat down beside her on a bench, some of the tension inside her started to soften. A light breeze lifted her hair and that helped calm her too. Or maybe it was the way Trip was holding her hand as if he were the one who needed steadying.

'I'm sorry I upset you. Again—'

'You didn't.'

'But something did,' he persisted. 'When I was taking that selfie.'

Trip watched her hands ball into fists. Up until that

moment, it had been a near flawless day, effortless in a way he had never imagined any relationship could be, and Lily had been happy and relaxed in a way that he had never seen before.

And then she wasn't.

He gritted his teeth. There had been so many days like this in the past when everything would be going well and then he would go too far. Take one risk too many. Forget to put on the brakes.

Except he hadn't done anything this time. It was Lily who had changed the mood. *Killed* the mood.

And he still wasn't sure why it had happened. One moment he had been leaning into her in the warm sunshine, feeling the light press of her body against his and thinking, Isn't this easy? The next she was demanding to go back to the house, her eyes shuttered, her body taut like an archer's bow.

'Maybe if you told me what it was, I could help—'

'You can't. You wouldn't understand.'

Her body tensed as it had before, almost as if she was bracing herself against some unseen threat.

'I might, and, even if I don't, I can still listen. Like you did.' Her face softened a fraction but then she shook her head.

'You wouldn't understand because you look like you. And I—I look like this.' Her hand moved to cover the slight bump on her nose.

He stared at her in confusion. 'Like what?'

'Like this.' Her voice turned sharp and she typed something into his phone and then held it out with a hand that shook slightly and he stared down at the screen, his brain jamming in shock and disgust as he read the headlines that accompanied photos of Lily as a child, then an adolescent, right through to almost present day. A few were the right side of jokey. Others were cruel. Some were just barbaric.

No wonder she hated having her photo taken. His anger was heavy and jagged beneath his ribs.

'Did your dad not stop these?'

'He did.' He heard the protective flare in her voice. 'He tried. But it's difficult. If you go after them, they just make out it was supposed to be a joke. And if you do get an apology, it just gives them a chance to resay or repost it all over again. It's just better to ignore them and not give them any oxygen. That's why there are fewer photos of me now. Because I'm careful.'

He felt sick. In other words, she kept a purposefully low profile. And he had dragged her into the spotlight.

'Look, Lily, these people are inhuman. That's why they're called trolls. You can't believe that normal people see you like this.'

'You did,' she said quietly. 'That first time we had lunch, you couldn't have made it any clearer that it was under duress.'

Was that what she had thought? His gaze moved from her high cheekbones down to her soft mouth and up to the bump on her nose. Her profile was not 'classically' beautiful, but she was a very beautiful woman. How could she not see that?

'I was hungover and you were snippy with me, so I was snippy back.'

'You only met me because you had to. You would

never go out to lunch with someone who looks like me ordinarily,' she countered.

'How could I? All the women I know look exactly the same.' Her face made it clear that he had simply proved her point. 'Not naturally. They've had fillers and "tweakments" and surgery. But just because you haven't, it doesn't mean these photos are an accurate representation of who you are.'

'How are they not accurate? They're not some AI-generated content. They're me.'

Shaking his head, he pocketed the phone and took hold of her hands. 'They're moments in time. It's not who you are.'

The shape of her mouth made his heart feel as if it were being squeezed in a vice.

'Is this where you tell me beauty is only skin-deep? Or in the eye of the beholder? Or that real beauty comes from within? That what matters is that I'm a good person?'

'That does matter. And you are a good person.'

'No, I'm not.' She pulled her hands free and as she wrapped her arms around her stomach, it seemed to transform her from hostile to vulnerable. 'I'm not. It's just that nobody knows.'

He stared at her in confusion. 'Then tell me,' he said finally. Because he wanted to know. To prove her wrong. To take that haunted look off her face.

Silence.

His throat was tight and aching. Silence was his nemesis. He had got better at managing it, mostly by tapping, but he was too scared that one tiny movement would send her spiralling away from him for ever. Or perhaps he had already lost her, he thought, gazing at her still, tense body.

'His name was Cameron.'

His shoulders stiffened. It was just a name but the way she said it made him want to seek him out and erase him from the face of the earth.

'Do I know him?'

She shook her head. 'I doubt it. We met when I came back from Oxford.' Her mouth twisted and she was silent for a moment. 'Sometimes I think if I'd never come here, it wouldn't have happened. I got complacent. I had such a wonderful time just being me that I started to believe I was okay. You know? Acceptable. But then I went back to the States and I realised I wasn't.'

'What happened?'

'I went to this fundraiser with my dad and I wore this dress and I thought I looked nice. Not incredible, just not—'

There was a tiny shake in her voice and he reached out and pulled her arm away from her waist, his hands seeking hers.

'Did he say something?' he said softly.

She heard the edge to his voice. 'Yes, but not in the way you're thinking.'

He felt his jaw tense. 'What did he do?'

'He was nice to me.' Her fingers tightened around his. 'I'd seen him around but we'd never talked, but I was sitting in this coffee shop a few days after the fundraiser, hiding really—' She gave him a small, bleak smile. 'He came over and told me that I was his hero. Then he sent this incredibly cutting message to this woman who'd posted a comment about my hair. Nobody had ever done that before. I was flattered.'

She took a deep breath. 'That was kind of our first date. We started seeing each other and then one Saturday he invited me and Lucas to this party at the Colvilles' house upstate.'

He nodded. He knew the house. Knew Ward Colville and his brother from school.

'At first it was fine. It was fun. Everyone was drinking and I did too, but I knew I had to get back because I had a breakfast meeting with a client. Only Cameron was too drunk to drive. We all were, except Lucas. I knew he didn't want to drive but I asked him anyway.'

He heard her swallow.

'Cameron put the music on real loud and he was singing and I forgot about Lucas because it felt like I was in a film. Only then suddenly there was this police car. And I wasn't worried because I knew Lucas hadn't been drinking. But what I didn't know was that Cameron had stolen the car Lucas was driving.'

Her hand moved to her face.

'Lucas was arrested.' The pain in her voice made his heart squeeze tight. 'We all got taken to the station. It was awful.'

'Why didn't I know about this?'

'My dad made it go away.' She hesitated. 'And it was about the time your mother and Charlie—'

He thought back to the days and weeks, the months after the accident. The whole world could have been on fire and he wouldn't have noticed.

'And Lucas?'

She bit her lip. 'He's not a lawbreaker. He was devastated. He wouldn't leave the house. He stopped composing and then one day I came back from work and he was lying on the floor in his bedroom and I couldn't wake him up.'

A tear ran down her cheek and he felt something wrench apart inside him. In answer to his earlier question, *this* was the worst that could happen. 'I'm so sorry, Lily.' He slid his arm around her waist and pulled her against him.

'Afterwards, he said it was an accident. He hadn't been sleeping well since the arrest and he was so anxious all the time. He told my mom and dad that he just wanted to stop all the noise in his head.'

He knew that feeling. When he was a child, it had been excruciating. At its worst, it had made sleeping, even sitting still, a torment.

'But my parents wanted to be sure. That's why they sent him to Switzerland. To the Galen.'

'It's a great clinic.' Pulling her closer, he kissed the top of her head. 'Carter's brother did rehab there. That's how I knew about Lucas. Carter asked me to go with him to collect his brother and I saw Lucas walk past a window just for a moment. I don't think I would even have noticed him, but he was holding a violin.'

Her face twisted.

'It was my fault. I knew Cameron was trouble. He was always telling lies. Stupid lies. Like once he left a restaurant without paying. He said it was a mistake, but he liked the danger. And I liked that he liked me because he was cool and good-looking and he validated me, made me feel beautiful. So I didn't care that he was dangerous. Because I'm shallow and selfish and not a good person.'

'Not true. You made a mistake and, sure, you have flaws, but you're only here with me because you care so much about Lucas. Because you know he struggles. But those struggles are part of him, *not* because of you or something you did. You're a good person. Better than good. Better than anyone I know, and, yes, that does make you beautiful. But so does this.' He touched the bump on her nose. 'And this.' He ran his finger along the curve of her jaw. 'And this.' Her eyes widened as he stroked a loose curl away from her cheek.

She had clearly wanted to believe him, but it was harder than people thought to let go of the bad things, the things people said or did and how they made you feel. That would mean hoping things could be better and hope was a dangerous thing and his throat thickened as she covered her face with a shaking hand. Finally, in a small, bruised voice, she said, 'You know, when we left the police station, I thought Cameron would apologise, but he didn't. I was angry with him and upset. I asked him how he could do something like that to me. And he laughed. He said that it was never serious. That he had "standards."'

The tears she had been holding back spilled over her cheeks now and, watching her attempts to control them, Trip pulled her close and held her close for a long time, letting her cry, pushing back against the hot burn of anger rising in his chest, wishing he had more than words to make her believe what he was saying.

Finally, her sobs subsided and she breathed out shakily. 'I'm sorry—'

'No, I'm sorry.' Ignoring her attempts to hide her face, he tilted up her chin. 'Listen to me, Lily. You were right, earlier. I wouldn't have asked you out to lunch, but not because I think you're not up to my standard. You were always so cool and aloof. I thought I wasn't up to yours. I thought—'

He fell silent, and, looking up at him, she felt her chest tighten. He looked taut and unhappy, as he had that time when he'd sat at the piano in Tuscany. Only back then there had been an edge to him, a challenge, as if he'd been testing her with the truth.

Now he looked tired, as if he was shouldering some huge unseen weight, and she thought about everything she'd had to keep to herself and carry alone. How hard it had been. How alone she had felt. But Trip had helped ease that burden. She had told him the truth, every ugly detail, and he had said she was beautiful. Made her feel beautiful.

'Thought what?' she said quietly. His fingers tightened infinitesimally so that she could feel his pulse beating against hers.

'I thought I would never be good enough. For anyone. But mostly for him. My father.'

There was another silence, and she made herself wait because she couldn't lead him where he needed to go. She could only hold his hand as tightly as he had held hers.

'But then I found these letters, and I was going to burn them. But they don't feel like they're mine to burn. I mean, he kept them for a reason.' He cleared his throat. 'You see, they're from a woman. Her name is Kerry. She was his mistress.'

Lily stared at him in shock. That couldn't be true. Theirs was a small, insular world but she hadn't heard so much as a whisper of scandal in relation to Henry and Alessandra Winslow's marriage.

'Was it serious?'

Trip shrugged. 'It went on for more than a decade, so, yeah, I guess it probably was. From the dates, I think they started seeing each other shortly after I was born.'

'When did you find the letters?' She hesitated. 'Was it before he…?'

He shook his head. His eyes were hard and flat. 'It was the day before I went to Ecuador.' He took a breath. 'It was why I went to Ecuador.'

The day he'd broken up with her. She could still remember it as if it had just happened. He had been angry, distant, spoiling for a fight and desperate to leave. And yet, in the end, she'd been the one to push him out of the door, too angry and hurt at the time to register the contradiction in his behaviour.

It was all too easy to imagine how he'd felt. Foremost shock, that sense of unreality and then the feeling of stupidity at not seeing what was right in front of you.

She felt Trip's eyes on her face. 'You know, the craziest part was that all I wanted to do was tell you. That's why I came to your apartment. But then when I saw you, I couldn't do it. I couldn't say the words out loud because I had this stupid, irrational need to protect him.'

'Not stupid or irrational. He was your father.'

'He was.' He was shaking his head as if to deny that fact. 'But sometimes, a lot of the time, he felt like an opponent. And he was always the reigning champion and I was the underdog and nothing I did could change that. And I spent all my life trying to be his equal, to be worthy—'

The ache in his voice bruised her skin.

'And then it turns out he wasn't this perfect, unattainable being. He was just a man with flaws and weaknesses. And I was so angry with him for lying to me, to my mother, to everyone. For making me feel irrelevant and not good enough.' His eyes were suddenly very blue. 'For dying.'

'Oh, Trip.' She slid both her arms around him, feeling his pain. Because it wasn't the trustees or the shareholders he wanted to impress, it was his father.

He pressed the heel of his hand against his forehead. 'Only I took it out on you because he wasn't there, and then I ran away because I knew if I stayed I'd do something stupid.' His mouth twisted. 'So I left and it happened anyway, because my head wasn't in the game. And the whole time I was there I kept imagining that look on his face. And then you'd pop into my head and it would disappear. I think that's why I kept thinking about you in Ecuador. You were a match for him.'

'You were too. That's why you clashed. Why Winslow's profits have gone up twenty per cent since you took over.'

'Until I got myself kidnapped.' The skin across his cheeks was taut. 'I proved him right.'

'You proved him wrong too. Multiple times.'

'But it was never enough.'

'I disagree. I think your father was old-fashioned enough to think that the oldest son should inherit, but I also know that he wouldn't have let his business be run by someone who wasn't good enough. You don't have to prove anything because he had proof. He chose you, not because he loved you, but because you are the best man for the job.'

Reaching out, he tucked her hair behind her ear. 'You know that, do you?' he said softly.

'I met your dad, remember? I worked with him. He had standards.' She paused and he knew that she was thinking about what that bastard Cameron had said to her at the police station, but then she gave him a small, tight smile. 'High standards, and he wasn't sentimental.'

'Not in the slightest.' His eyes fixed on hers and there was an expression on his face that made her scalp prickle.

'And what about you? Am I the best man for you?'

'Yes, you're the best man for me.' The only man. Her heart twitched and, panicking at the truth and stupidity of that thought, she rolled her eyes and quickly added, 'Or you'll do for now anyway.'

He smiled a little.

'Is that right?' He stared at her steadily. 'I thought you weren't going to do this.'

'Do what?'

'Talk. Hold my hand. Offer me a shoulder to cry on. Give me the best version of yourself.' He reached out to touch her cheek, his thumb tracing the line of her mouth. 'What changed your mind?'

Her heart was racing, mind turning over his words, over and over, not because she didn't know the answer, but because she did. He had changed her mind. Changed her. Changed everything. Rearranged the world into a place of possibility, filled it with light and laughter and love.

She felt dizzy, drunk, but she wasn't drunk. She was in love. Helplessly, frantically, impossibly in love with Trip.

'Oxford,' she managed. 'Being here made me realise that we're in this together.'

It was the truth, part of it anyway. But there would be other, better times to say more. Better than now when the torrent of emotions stampeding through her were making it hard to sit upright.

His eyes were very blue.

'We are. And I meant what I said before. I wasn't expecting what happened between us to happen, but the truth is that I've never wanted any woman like I wanted you. Like I want you, now, all the time and not in spite of the fact that you're different from those other women, but *because* you're different.

'You are beautiful, Lily, and I don't mean on the inside. I think you're sexy as hell and where you see flaws, I see authenticity. Because a diamond with a flaw is

more beautiful than some perfect manufactured gem-
stone. That's me trying to be poetic, just so you know.'

She smiled. 'It's a pity the shareholders aren't here.'

'I don't care about the shareholders.' He frowned as if
he was surprised to find that was true. 'I care about you.
You're with me now, and I'm going to keep you safe. I
won't let anyone get close enough to hurt you. I promise.'

It wasn't love but it was enough for now.

CHAPTER NINE

THE SUNLIGHT WAS weaker here in England than Italy, Lily thought as she sat down in front of the dressing-table mirror. But it was still bright enough to make sunblock necessary. Glancing over her shoulder, she massaged the cream into her back. She could, of course, just wait for Trip, but the last time she had asked for his help they had spent the rest of the day in bed.

Desire curled inside her at the memory and her gaze moved to the bathroom where Trip was showering. But it wasn't desire that had pushed them into each other's arms on that park bench.

Something had changed. It wasn't just sex any more. It felt like a relationship. He had told her he cared about her, that he would keep her safe. Nothing had ever meant more to her than knowing Trip had her back.

It had been one of the hardest things she had ever done, showing him those photos of herself. Her heart had been racing, hands shaking. She had never told anyone how it had made her feel. Never wanted to. Had been too scared to, because then they might see her in that way and be repulsed by her 'ugliness'.

But when Trip had taken her hand it had all come

pouring out of her and he hadn't looked at her in disgust. And just as momentous had been Trip's confession to her. His father's infidelity had been shocking, but more shocking still, more devastating to her, was finally understanding the full extent of his insecurities in relation to Henry. How he had protected himself by pushing back against his father's indifference and disappointment, presenting an image of himself as cool and emotionally indifferent. She knew now that he was not that man. Not with her, anyway.

Maybe that was why she had felt a peace that was deeper than she had ever known.

As long as she didn't think about the future, she still felt at peace now. Some of the time anyway, she thought, her breath catching as Trip strolled back into the bedroom with a fluid grace that made it impossible to look away.

'So, what do you want to do today?'

'You choose.'

'I was hoping you'd say that.' He grinned. 'Let's go for a punt.' His gaze flicked over her bare back. 'But first…' Her pulse jerked as his warm hand slid over her shoulder. 'You missed a bit here.'

'Is that right?'

'I wouldn't lie to you,' he said softly, tracing a lazy, sensual path down to the swell of her bottom. 'Not about anything.'

His eyes met hers in the mirror and she stared back at him dizzily.

Before yesterday, she would have told herself it was just words, but she could see the truth written across his face—no, not written, she corrected herself. It was deeper than that. As if it were cut into him like letters into stone.

And the strange thing was that in the past she had hated to be looked at. But here in Oxford, she liked it when Trip looked at her in that fierce, focused, incisive way of his that told her he liked what he saw. Maybe that was why being here felt as if she were in a dream, she thought, but then he leaned down and his mouth found hers and she had no thoughts for anything but him and as her hunger flared, white and brighter than any sun, she reached for the towel around his waist, reached for him.

Punting was a good choice, she thought, two hours later as they took turns to push the flat-bottomed boat through the rippling waters of the Cherwell. Away from the centre, it was quiet and cool on the river. Now, as she lay back against the cushions, gazing up at the sky, it was easy to feel outside time, adrift.

And Trip was great company. Smart, funny, curious and he had that incredible energy and excitement. But it was when he talked about his plans for the business that she started to realise that he was a lot more than just a pretty face. A whole lot more.

Another punt was gliding into view now. Not a couple but a group of women taking photos of each other. She felt an instant flutter of panic as they glanced over at Trip but then her gaze snagged on the magazine one of the women was holding. On the cover, next to a photo of some soap star who'd split from her husband, was the same photo Trip had shown her back in New York, the one from the auction. No doubt because it was one of the few in existence of the two of them together.

So far.

'Hey...' Trip turned towards her, and she felt her stomach swoop upwards by the curving uptilt of his mouth. 'Where'd you go?'

'Nowhere,' she lied, watching as the women disappeared. 'I was just thinking about how different it is here from New York.'

'Are you missing it?' There was an edge to his voice that hadn't been there before.

No, she thought, but as she opened her mouth to reply there was a crash and the punt shuddered sideways. Gripping the sides, she looked over her shoulder to where another punt occupied by a couple had rearended them.

'Sorry.' The man was getting to his feet, grimacing. 'That was my fault,' he said in that clipped, English accent, his cheeks flushed pink. 'I wasn't looking where I was going.'

'It's fine.' Trip smiled easily. 'Really. No harm, no foul.' To Lily, he murmured, 'Don't worry, we've got this,' his hand squeezing hers.

The woman in the punt was smiling and crying a little. 'He just proposed.' She held out her hand and the small diamond solitaire winked in the sunlight. 'And I said yes,' she added unnecessarily.

'Congratulations!' Trip turned to Lily and there was a glitter of excitement in his eyes that made her pulse hum with happiness. 'We actually got engaged earlier this month, didn't we, darling?'

'Oh, congratulations.' The woman leant forward, smiling at Lily. 'Can I see your ring?'

Beside her, Lily felt Trip shift his weight as he reached to take her hand. He was smiling too, but as she stared down at the glittering band on her finger, she felt a lump form in her throat. The jewels in her ring trumped the other woman's in size and worth, but they felt cheap and gaudy in comparison. Because of course they were not a declaration of love. Her ring was simply an expensive but impersonal prop selected by Trip, or more likely Lazlo, to persuade the world that their engagement was real.

And it wasn't that she didn't know that to be the case, but seeing this couple, feeling their love and hope and excitement, was a crushing reminder that her relationship with Trip was a sham.

She shivered as the sun momentarily disappeared behind a cloud. She couldn't let herself think about that now. 'I love the shape of yours,' she said quickly, ignoring the ache in her chest.

'It's beautiful,' Trip added smoothly. 'But I'm sure you've got better things to do than talk to us. Congratulations again—'

As the couple moved off downstream he met her gaze.

Reaching out, he touched her cheek lightly. 'You know, I don't know why you were ever worried about getting people to believe in us. For a moment there, even I believed you. And the shareholders are going to believe you too.' He smiled then, one of those miraculous smiles that made the earth tilt on its axis. But for once it was hard to smile back.

And that was what mattered, she thought, over the dark ache in her heart. She knew if she sat there, leaning into Trip's warmth, living the lie, she might shatter.

'We should be getting back.'

The punt wobbled alarmingly as she jerked to her feet, and she would have lost her balance if Trip hadn't grabbed her wrist.

'Don't.' She shook him off. 'What's the point of being in disguise if you're going to draw attention to us?'

Grabbing the pole, he steadied the punt calmly. 'Be fair, Lily. You're the one who nearly capsized us.'

He was right.

And the stupid thing was that she didn't care about anyone noticing them. Didn't even care about the paparazzi. Had never cared less, in fact. Her eyes snagged on the dazzling diamond and sapphires on her finger and everything inside her rolled sideways as if she herself were about to capsize. Yesterday, and this morning, she had felt so close to him, so safe, so known. And she had thought she knew *him*. Had thought that things had shifted, changed in some intangible but fundamental way—

'Lily—'

The gentleness in his voice was so unexpected that she was suddenly close to tears. 'Don't do that. Don't say my name,' she said shakily.

The sun had slipped behind a cloud so that his eyes looked like bruises. Watching his face stiffen, she wished she could turn back time to when it was just the two of them in this fantasy he'd created.

She sat down, turning her face away from him. It

didn't matter that he had brought her to her safe place, or that he had shown her the man beneath the teasing smile and the careless manner. The beautiful, bright day was ruined. Their lies had sent the sun scurrying behind the clouds.

Quite suddenly she wished she had fallen into the river and sunk to the mud at the bottom, where there was no sunlight and Trip's smile would be a blurred, indistinct memory.

They made their way back to the house in silence, but as soon as they were inside the bedroom, Trip rounded on her.

'What is going on? Lily, what's the matter? You can't just give me the silent treatment. Talk to me.'

Trip's flawless face was creased into a frown that was a shock after days of light and laughter.

'You didn't propose,' she said quietly.

His frown deepened, his frustration palpable now beneath his confusion. 'Because it would have felt weird. It wasn't that kind of engagement. But that doesn't suddenly mean something just because we met some couple on a punt who did the whole down on bended knee schtick.'

A couple who were in love, she thought dully. A couple who weren't performing a part.

His expression shifted, softened. 'Look, I'm sorry I didn't propose.' He took a step closer, reaching for her hand. His handsome face so familiar, so necessary now, and it would be so easy to just accept his apology.

'But you have a ring and if you want we can post

some pictures to show it off. And I can get Lazlo to send over some venue ideas for the ceremony.'

It was like waking from a dream. He was talking to her as if she were a colleague or a client. It jarred, unfairly so, because Trip hadn't romanced her into this relationship. For him, their engagement was a pragmatic, spur-of-the-moment solution to a business dilemma. There was never any need for him to personalize his love, because he didn't love her.

But in her newly loved-up state, she had let herself forget that he had needed a wife, needed her to improve his image.

Or had she chosen to ignore it? She pressed her hand against her chest to quell the queasiness that question provoked. Because she had done that once before with appalling consequences.

Better to face it head-on.

'It doesn't matter now,' she said slowly.

His eyes narrowed on her face. 'What do you mean?'

She flinched inwardly, but continued. 'In Italy you said that there was an agenda, a right time to announce our engagement. I think this would be the perfect time to announce our separation.'

He was looking at her as if she were an imposter. Someone playing the part of Lily Dempsey. 'I don't understand. Why are you talking about separating? We haven't even picked a date for the wedding. Look, it's going to be fine, Lily. Everyone is going to love you and when they see us together they won't suspect a thing. They'll all think we're madly in love—'

For a few seconds she remembered how he had comforted her while she'd cried. How tightly he had held her hand as he'd told her about his father's affair. She thought she would throw up if she asked the question, but she wasn't going to make the same mistake twice.

'But we're not, are we?' She took a deep breath. 'Or, rather, you're not.'

Heart hammering against her ribs, she waited, watching as he ran a hand across his face. Hiding his eyes, she thought, her stomach lurching as she saw the implication of her words hit home. He looked stunned, and even before he started to speak, she knew that her feelings were not and would never be returned.

And it hurt. It hurt so badly she wanted to curl into a ball around the ache in her chest. She felt small and foolish, as she had so many times in her life.

He was shaking his head. 'I don't—I'm not—'

His stumbling, uncharacteristic inarticulateness told her everything she needed to know.

She felt as if she were slipping underwater. 'Of course.' Her nails bit into the palms of her hands. Just hours earlier she had felt cocooned and needed at the heart of his life, but she wasn't in his heart. He didn't want a real relationship and she couldn't be in this fake one. Couldn't be this diminished version of herself, not even for Trip. 'Can I leave it to you to make a statement? You know how to explain things.'

He moved to stand by the window and she took a step closer to the door, both of them moving like actors blocking a performance. Because that was what they were. That was all they could ever be, and accepting that gave her the willpower to stay strong.

* * *

'If that's what you want.' His voice was flat, distant.

It wasn't, but she didn't want to just be a solution to a problem.

'What I want is to be loved. What I want is to truly share my life with someone, not pretend to share it with someone just to please a bunch of shareholders I've never met. And I suppose I should thank you, because you made me realise I deserve better than this. I deserve more. I deserve someone who loves me.'

'You do,' he said hoarsely. 'Look, Lily—'

She cut across him. That he had so easily given in, given her up was like a spear lancing her heart. But she couldn't stand here and listen to him tell her that he was fond of her. 'All I ask is that you hold off making any announcement about us until after I've told my family.'

'Will Lucas be okay?'

Lucas. Without him, she would never have agreed to this engagement. But she couldn't use him to stay with Trip now, couldn't use love in that way. And oddly, Trip had made her see that she didn't need to feel responsible for her brother. She would protect him, but her family was strong and they would stand together. As for herself, no troll could inflict pain that would match that of staying with Trip and knowing that it would never be real.

There was a sharp beat of silence and then he nodded. She took a deep breath. 'I'll just get my things—'

She held her breath, hoping, praying that he would stop her, stop this from happening. But after a few beats of silence he said stiffly, 'I'll get Lazlo to organise a jet.'

'You don't need to do that.'

He glanced towards the window. 'I want to. In fact, I insist on it. The main airports are probably under siege by the paps and I said I'd keep you safe.'

His matter-of-fact tone made her flinch inside. The last time he had spoken those words, his voice had been soft and tender. Now it was as if he were sitting in his office, dictating a letter to his PA.

But then this had always been about business for him, she thought, her pulse pounding hard in her head. Keeping control of Winslow. He had never promised love.

'I'll wait downstairs. Come and find me when you're ready to leave.'

Her legs felt as though they were no longer solid beneath her. It was unimaginable to be without him, but it would be worse, so much worse to marry him and then have to wait for it to end.

'Thank you.' Clenching her fists to stop her hands shaking, she lifted her chin. 'Goodbye, Trip. I hope it all works out for you—'

He didn't look at her. Just continued to stare at the window and then abruptly he turned and walked away. She watched his back, willing him to turn around and come striding back to her. She pictured him pulling her in his arms and telling her that he needed her in his life for ever.

But this wasn't a fairy tale, so instead he kept walking and she kept standing there, her heart breaking, shattering inside her ribs.

CHAPTER TEN

LEANING FORWARD TO rest his elbows against the kitchen counter, Trip stared blankly at his laptop screen. It was good news, the best in fact. Winslow had just signed a deal with the world's biggest fitness tracker. It was his project and it had sent share prices soaring. His email was clogged with congratulatory messages from trustees and shareholders. He had no need of a wife to improve his image.

But there was nobody to share the moment.

His chest felt as if it had been hollowed out with a spoon. He was alone.

Not officially. Not publicly. Not yet.

That would happen tomorrow. If he could find the right words.

It was two hours since he'd walked out of their bedroom, and it felt like a lifetime, but he could hardly rush her. So he was giving her space even though he still couldn't believe that it had ended this way. That it had ended at all.

It made no sense for her to react as she had. Everything had been going perfectly. There had been a smoothness to every second that he knew logically was beyond her control and yet her being there seemed to give everything a tensile certainty. But, at some point between stepping on and off the punt, it had all fallen apart.

Don't say my name.

That was what she'd said to him, and it had been a shock, like a physical blow, because he knew how it felt to hear her say his name and he'd thought she felt the same. Only her voice had had that snap of some last thread fraying, as if she'd grown tired of pretending.

And that had hurt, so he'd done what he always did when something pushed him away. He'd pushed back.

He could still see the expression on her face, that mix of shock and hurt, and he knew that was on him. But Lily had caught him off balance talking about separating and then suddenly...

The floor tilted beneath his feet as if he were suffering from vertigo. It was the same feeling as before when she'd told him she loved him in so many words. When she had stripped herself bare of all her protective layers. He knew what it must have cost her to do so, and he had done nothing. Said nothing. Nothing coherent anyway. He had just stood there, watching her try to hold herself together.

His hands clenched into fists and he slammed them against the counter, welcoming the sting of pain because it took the edge off the ache tearing through his chest and splitting his heart.

But what was he supposed to say? Their 'engagement' was never about love. Hell, he wasn't sure he even knew what love was. He understood the concept, but in his family love was expressed primarily through material support. There was financial security on an unimaginable scale but affection, emotional support and that intuitive understanding were absent.

Right up until he'd tricked Lily onto that plane.

She had fought with him, challenged him, comforted him, and been at his side during one of the hardest periods of his entire life. But he hadn't been prepared for her loving him.

Or for how much he loved her.

And that was when he realised why he was hurting so much. Why he felt sick and split and broken and empty. He loved Lily.

Wanted her, needed her, loved her with an intensity that matched the surge of blood beating from his heart.

Turning, he walked swiftly through the house. The door to the bedroom was open and he strode in, his heart hammering in his throat.

'Lily, I—'

He stopped. The bedroom was silent and empty. So was the bathroom. So were all the other rooms in the house and the garden. He checked and double-checked, retracing his steps, panic swelling inside him but no amount of searching could change the facts.

Lily was gone. His gaze snagged on something bright and glittering on the bedside table. But she had left the ring.

It was starting to rain. Tugging her jacket around her shoulders, Lily glanced dully up at the clouds, then crossed the street.

She had taken the red-eye from Heathrow to JFK. Nobody had given her a second glance. The steward had come by with the trolley but the effort of choosing, of talking, had overwhelmed her. Instead, she had turned towards the window and wrapped her arms around her waist to stop her from disintegrating and, surprisingly, she had fallen asleep instantly and slept until the early morning light seeped through the window to press against her eyelids.

Waking, she had remembered all of it and her misery had been caustic. In some horrible parody of her flight to Italy, she hadn't wanted to leave the plane. But she couldn't stay there for ever, and finally she had got to her feet and made her way down the aisle.

She'd had a momentary wobble as she'd walked through the terminal. It had felt so final, so absolute. The taxi ride back to the city had been a welcome diversion but she'd made the driver drop her off a few streets from her apartment. She'd wanted to set the pace for herself. Not just be driven up and deposited on the pavement.

And it was okay, walking through the quiet, familiar streets with her keys clutched in her hand like a talisman. Just putting one step in front of the other gave her something to focus on, and with each step she was one step closer to home. One step closer to the life she needed to start living now.

As she turned the corner, her feet faltered as she spotted a group of young women weaving their way along the pavement towards her. But they were drunk and, frankly, she was past feeling worried about anyone recognising her. Past feeling anything.

The memory of Trip walking out of the room without so much as a backwards glance made her chest feel as if it were a gaping wound. That love could hurt so much was astonishing, but she couldn't undo what had been done, and she wouldn't even if it were an option.

She couldn't let herself think about that now. It would fade in time, become bearable. And in the meantime she had a career she loved, a family she loved even more, and friends to distract her.

She had reached her street and, picturing her small, cosy apartment, she felt a rush of relief and gratitude. She would be safe there. She could heal and then she would face the world.

'It's her—'

'Lily—'

Glancing up, Lily felt her breath stall. Men with cameras and microphones were uncurling themselves from car seats, staggering to their feet, their eyes hard and flat as they started to run towards her.

Her feet froze and for a moment everything went into slow motion as she stared at them, panic swelling inside her. If she hadn't been so distracted she might have noticed them, been more prepared, but she wasn't prepared at all and, before she even had time to think of a Plan B, she found herself surrounded by a pack of paparazzi and reporters shouting questions.

Somewhere beyond the jostling men she heard the roar of an engine and the screech of brakes. Then footsteps, heavy, urgent. There were more of them.

'No comment,' she said, holding one hand in front of her face, trying to block out their lenses and their questions as she looked for an exit. But there were too many of them. They were like a dark cloud smothering her.

She blinked into a sudden glare of light. But it wasn't the flash of a camera, it was sunlight. Breathing out shakily, she saw Trip shouldering his way through the pack. His blue eyes were blazing with a fury that made most of the paparazzi step backwards. Behind him a team of men in dark suits and even darker glasses were creating a human barricade in front of the remaining reporters.

'Are you okay?' Trip was by her side, the blaze of anger softening as he stared down at her.

'What are you doing here?'

'I promised to keep you safe,' he said, his shoulders rising and falling on a deep breath and, reaching down, he scooped her into his arms and carried her and didn't stop until they were inside her apartment.

'You can put me down now,' she said stiffly. 'And then you can let yourself back out.'

Trip let go of her and she walked quickly away.

'I'm sorry I upset you. Again.'

He stared over to where she was looking at her phone, or pretending to look at her phone. There was a tension to her bowed head that made him think that she was seeing nothing on the screen. That her whole body was arrowed in on his position in the room.

'I didn't mean to. I didn't want to. I never want to upset you.'

The stiffness in her shoulders moved to her spine but she didn't respond and, for a fraction of a second, he almost turned and left. But then he thought about how she had stayed with him after they'd argued, how she had let him talk. Listened. Comforted him. And so he tried again, because he had to. Because this time he couldn't leave. He didn't want to.

'And I didn't take you to Oxford so that people would see us together,' he said quietly. 'I wouldn't do that—'

Her shoulders were still rigid but her eyes floated over to his. 'No, because tricking people, pushing your own agenda—that's not your way of doing things, is it?'

The tiredness in her voice pierced him. It made her sound so much older than twenty-eight, and yet younger too. Like a frightened child. He took a breath.

'It was, before. Back in New York. I felt trapped and I was angry and I didn't think about what you wanted. I was only thinking about myself. But that's why I asked you to come with me to Oxford. Because I know you loved being there and I thought it would make you happy.'

Her eyes found his. 'I was happy.'

Was. Past tense. He felt the rush of fear and panic that had swamped him as he walked back downstairs from the empty bedroom, that same sense of being trapped inside a shrinking tomb. 'Why did you leave? I thought you were upstairs, but you were gone. And you didn't take the plane.'

'You don't get to tell me what to do.' Lily wrapped her arms in front of her chest like a shield, walling herself off, shutting him out.

'You could have been hurt.'

'I already have been,' she said slowly. 'I think we're done here, Trip.'

'I'm not finished.' He looked at her impatiently. She was as stubborn as she was beautiful.

'Well, I am. I have nothing to say to you, Trip,' she managed to say, 'and you said everything you needed to say yesterday—'

'But that's just it. I didn't.' Trip stared at her. His heart was still beating out of time from seeing her surrounded by reporters like a deer cornered by hounds. 'I didn't know what I thought. One minute you were saying all this stuff about wanting to separate and the next you were saying you loved me.'

'That was yesterday.'

'Lily, please.'

The tightness in his voice made everything inside her roll sideways like a capsizing boat. But this was what Trip did. He rushed headlong in where angels feared to tread. To Ecuador or into a pack of baying paparazzi.

'What? I know you. I know how you think. How you react, how you overreact because that's who you are. It's what you do, it's what you did before. Only instead of going to Ecuador, you turn up with a bunch of bodyguards and make out that it's because of a promise you're keeping.'

'I did make you a promise. And yes, you're right, this is what I do, but I'm not that person any more, Lily. You changed me. You made me look at myself, look at the person I was.'

He took a step closer. 'I've been so angry for so long.

Angry with myself, but mostly angry with my father. When I found those letters I didn't deal with how it made me feel, I just ran away. You made me realise that I needed to deal with that anger. Or I'd ruin the future.'

'You don't need to worry about that. I saw the headlines. Congratulations. I'm sure the shareholders are more than happy for you to run the business now.'

'I'm not talking about Winslow, Lily.' The fierceness in his voice made her flinch. 'I'm talking about our future.'

'We don't have a future.' Her chest squeezed tight. 'I told you, I'm not going to marry a man who doesn't love me.'

'No, you're not. You're going to marry a man who's madly, helplessly, completely and utterly in love with you.' His voice was choked with tears. 'Because I love you, Lily Dempsey. I love you, and I need you in my life, not just in my heart, but by my side.'

She watched in astonishment as he dropped to one knee and took her hands in his.

'So will you be my wife? Will you marry me?'

'You're proposing.'

Trip nodded. 'Say yes, please.'

'Yes,' she said softly, her tears falling freely now because they were tears of happiness, and then he was pulling her down and his mouth was on hers. They kissed hungrily, kissed until the pain of parting was forgotten.

'You know nobody will know the difference,' Lily said shakily, searching his face, seeing the love there, feeling it radiating through his body to hers.

His hands slid down over her body, holding her

steady, steadying himself. 'We will,' he said softly. 'We'll know. And I wanted, I *want*, to give you a new ring to show you how different it is for me now. But I didn't want to rush into anything. And I don't have to. Not when we have forever together.'

And he pulled her against him, breathing in her scent, the scent of this woman who was everything he needed in the world.

* * * * *

Did you fall in love with Reclaimed with a Ring*?*
Then why not try the other instalments in
The Diamond Club *series?*

Baby Worth Billions *by Lynne Graham*
Pregnant Princess Bride *by Caitlin Crews*
Greek's Forbidden Temptation *by Millie Adams*
Italian's Stolen Wife *by Lorraine Hall*
Heir Ultimatum *by Michelle Smart*
His Runaway Royal *by Clare Connelly*
Stranded and Seduced *by Emmy Grayson*

Available now!

HARLEQUIN
Reader Service

Enjoyed your book?

Try the perfect subscription for Romance readers and get more great books like this delivered right to your door.

See why over 10+ million readers have tried Harlequin Reader Service.

Start with a Free Welcome Collection with free books and a gift—valued over $20.

Choose any series in print or ebook. See website for details and order today:

TryReaderService.com/subscriptions